Praise for Frances O'Roark Dowell's quilting novel, BIRDS IN THE AIR

"An uplifting story of a woman finding her way in a small town, this will delight experienced quilters and novice crafters alike. Author Dowell is best known for her YA fiction, and her experience crafting narratives around the power of female friendships transfers easily to more mature subject matter. With buoyant prose and an uplifting message, this will appeal to fans of Mary Simses and Erin McGraw." ***—Booklist***

"A truly enjoyable read! Quilters will relive their own first patchwork steps along with Emma as she searches for her place in a new community. Non-quilters will experience vicariously Emma's discovery of the power of quilts to connect, heal, and restore the soul." ***—Marianne Fons***

"What a delightful book! Frances weaves a story with characters that remind us of people we know in our every day lives – so relatable. As I read, I was transported out of my chair and into the town of Sweet Anne's Gap and the lives of the quilters that I can understand so well. The surprise ending makes me hope that Emma Byrd's story will continue on and become a series of lovely quilting stories." ***—Annie Smith, SimpleArts.com***

"Birds in the Air is a great book and quilt block -- it is as unusual as liking the book and the movie! It was such a pleasurable read." ***—Kathy Mathews, ChicagoNow***

MARGARET GOES MODERN

Also by Frances O'Roark Dowell

BIRDS IN THE AIR

* * *

THE SECRET LANGUAGE OF GIRLS

THE KIND OF FRIENDS WE USED TO BE

THE SOUND OF YOUR VOICE, ONLY REALLY FAR AWAY

* * *

ANYBODY SHINING

CHICKEN BOY

DOVEY COE

FALLING IN

THE SECOND LIFE OF ABIGAIL WALKER

SHOOTING THE MOON

TEN MILES PAST NORMAL

TROUBLE THE WATER

WHERE I'D LIKE TO BE

* * *

PHINEAS L. MCGUIRE . . . BLASTS OFF!

PHINEAS L. MCGUIRE . . . ERUPTS!

PHINEAS L. MCGUIRE . . . GETS COOKING!

PHINEAS L. MCGUIRE . . . GETS SLIMED!

* * *

SAM THE MAN & THE CHICKEN PLAN

SAM THE MAN & THE RUTABAGA PLAN

SAM THE MAN & THE DRAGON VAN PLAN

MARGARET GOES MODERN

AND OTHER STORIES

FRANCES O'ROARK DOWELL

Margaret Goes Modern.

Milton Falls Media, Inc.
2608 Erwin Road, #148-152
Durham, N.C. 27705
www.miltonfallsmedia.com

For information about purchasing Milton Falls Media books, please write to the publisher at: sales@miltonfallsmedia.com.

Cover Design: Jenny Zemanek
Seedlings Design Studio | www.seedlingsonline.com

Publisher's Cataloging-In-Publication Data
(Prepared by The Donohue Group, Inc.)

Names: Dowell, Frances O'Roark.
Title: Margaret goes modern, and other stories / Frances O'Roark Dowell.
Description: Durham, N.C. : Milton Falls Media, [2017]
Identifiers: Identifiers: LCCN 2017918187 |
ISBN 9781945354038 | ISBN 9781945354045 (ebook)

Subjects: LCSH: Women--Fiction. | Quiltmakers--Fiction. | Mothers and daughters--Fiction. | Sisters--Fiction. | Loss (Psychology)--Fiction. | LCGFT: Short stories.
Classification: LCC PS3604.O939 M37 2017 (print) |
LCC PS3604.O939 (ebook) | DDC 813/.6--dc23

Library of Congress Control Number: 2017918187

Contents

For Kristin Esser

Persimmon Moon

Amanda has counted twenty-seven pumpkins in all, and twenty-seven seems like a lucky number. It's not a prime number, but two is prime and so is seven, and in Amanda's opinion, twenty-seven is close enough to a prime number to be considered lucky, if you consider prime numbers lucky, which she does.

"We could have used thirty," her sister Lucy says when Amanda walks into the kitchen to report the news. Lucy is carefully measuring vanilla into a mixing bowl. Lucy is always carefully measuring something into a mixing bowl, and she doesn't believe in lucky numbers. There is only one bit of superstition Lucy holds onto, and it's the worst kind, the kind that leaves her stuck exactly where she is.

"But twenty-seven is good," Amanda insists, "and the pumpkins are all perfect and almost ready to be picked. Vonnie said she wanted the pies for the Harvest Festival next Saturday, and she'll have them, and we'll have lots of lovely money in exchange."

"Not lots of money," Lucy says, cracking an egg into a blue ceramic bowl. "A little bit of money. Not enough money."

"But we'll be on our way to having enough money." Amanda leans across the counter and steals a piece of shaved bittersweet chocolate from the cutting board. All this money talk is making her nervous, and when Amanda gets nervous, she eats. She eats a lot in the fall, because fall is when their money gets tight. Fall is when the crowds at the farmers market begin to thin, as does Lucy's cutting garden. The asters and toad lilies are still blooming, and so are the Russian sage and the colchicum.

But now Amanda and Lucy can sleep until six-thirty on market days, whereas in the summer they had to be up at four to have enough time to clip and arrange the abundance of flowers the garden provided.

"I think we should plant an apple tree out front," Amanda says. "We could sell apple pies this time of year, or jars of applesauce. We could make apple crumble. People like apples."

"By the time an apple tree matures, we will have sold the house and moved to an apartment on Barkley Street," Lucy says. "We'll both work in horrible office jobs and spend all day on computers."

Both sisters shudder. They have never had a computer in their house nor ever desired one. A few years ago, Lucy broke down and bought a smartphone because businesses that carried her baked goods insisted they be able to reach her via email or text, but that was as far into the computer age as either sister has ever been willing to venture. Amanda believes strongly that any device with a screen is dangerous and possibly soul-sucking, although sometimes she sneaks over to her best friend Emily's house to watch black-and-white movies on Friday nights. She makes sure to sit as far away from Emily's television as she can, just to be on the safe side.

"Well, if we're not going to plant an apple tree, why don't we plant blueberries? Everyone loves blueberry preserves."

Lucy sighs, and Amanda doesn't push any further. Besides, she already knows about blueberry bushes, how they take three or four years to mature. She and Lucy don't have three or four years. They are three or four months from running through the last of their inheritance, and when that happens they will have no choice but to put their house on the market. The irony is, Amanda thinks, that if they sold their house, they'd have enough money to stay in their house. More than one realtor has come to sniff around, dropping hints about what a cottage as charming as theirs might bring from an eager buyer.

Lucy pours the eggs into the mixing bowl and begins whisking in a way that seems aggressive to Amanda, as though her sister has a bone to pick with her batter. "Your cake is going to turn out tough if you don't lighten up," she says, and Lucy stops and takes a deep breath.

"Amanda, I know you don't want to talk about this, but we have to. If we don't do something, we'll have to put the house up for sale in January. I've looked at the budget every way possible, but even if we had a hundred pumpkins for a hundred pies, even if our sunflowers bloomed through the winter, we'd come up short."

Amanda sits down at the kitchen table. She wishes she had a cup of peppermint tea. She wishes her cat Gretel was curled purring in her lap, and she wishes she knew how to knit. It would be so lovely to drink peppermint tea and knit with a cat curled up purring in her lap, not having to worry about leaving the only house she has ever lived in or ever wanted to live in.

"I was born in this house," she says to Lucy, and Lucy rolls her eyes. Lucy turned thirty-two in May, and Amanda thinks that's much too old to still be in the eye-rolling stage of life.

"Well, the way things are going, you won't die in this house," Lucy says. "At least that's some consolation."

"It's not," Amanda says and has to stop from pouting. She herself has recently turned thirty, and she feels that pouting past age twenty-nine is undignified.

Lucy walks around from behind the counter and takes a seat across the table from Amanda. Wisps of ash-blonde hair have escaped from her ponytail and curl delicately around her face, softening its sharp angles. Amanda has never been able to understand how a woman who spends half of her day baking can stay so thin. It must be that she spends the other half of her day out in the garden with a hoe in her hand.

"Honey, you have to listen to me," Lucy says, reaching her hand across the table and putting it on top of Amanda's. "It's time. If you want to stay in this house, you've got to start selling your quilts."

Amanda pulls her hand back and shakes her head as hard as she can. "I don't quilt for money. Not any more."

"You had one bad experience, and really, it wasn't that bad." Lucy's tone makes it clear she thinks her sister is over-reacting. Is always over-reacting. "And you can do things differently this time. You could find another way."

"I can't make a quilt with colors that don't speak to me. I can't use other people's patterns or follow their ideas. Melinda Blanchette wanted stars, and I was in the wrong place to do stars. And she wanted me to use yellow at a time when yellow was the farthest thing from my mind. It was an awful experience."

"But Melinda loved those stars, whether you did or not," Lucy insists. "And she still talks about that quilt every time I see her at the market. She's got a daughter getting married in the spring, and she wants you to make her a Double Wedding Ring quilt. How hard would that be?"

"That would be — impossible." Amanda is near tears. "I can't think of anything more terrible."

"And you know what?" Lucy continues as though she hasn't heard her sister. "Every time I stop by the inn, Vonnie tells me someone has asked to buy that quilt you gave her. You know how she has it on the armchair by the fireplace? All people have to do is touch it — just lean back against it — and suddenly they're happy. All their burdens disappear."

Amanda nods. "It's a healing quilt. I made it for Vonnie when she was going through chemo. Of course it makes them feel better."

"My point is, you could sell all the quilts you wanted through Vonnie. And you could charge whatever you wanted."

"It doesn't work when you're doing it for money."

"What doesn't work?"

Amanda leans forward and whispers. "The magic."

Lucy leans forward and whispers. "Who cares? People want to buy your quilts, and we need their money."

Amanda is quiet for a moment. What she's about to say isn't fair, and she knows it, but it's the only card she has to play. "If we need money so badly, marry John. With both of your incomes and the money from my dressmaking, we'd have enough. John loves the house, so we wouldn't have to sell it."

Lucy's face darkens. "You know I can't."

"I know you can. And I know you want to. And he wants to. And you'd be so happy together!"

"I need to put the cake in the oven," Lucy says, standing.

"So that's it? That's the end of the discussion?"

"End of discussion."

"You have a degree in biochemistry!" Amanda is standing now, too. "How can a person with a degree in biochemistry be so superstitious?"

"How many times do I have to say this?" Lucy is leaning down to turn on the oven and doesn't even bother to look at Amanda. "I am only superstitious in this one regard. If anything happened to you because I got married, I wouldn't be able to live with myself. I'd have to jump into the river with rocks in my pockets."

"Nothing would happen."

"Aunt Lucinda said it would, and I believe her."

Amanda can't listen any more. She stomps out of the kitchen and heads for her sewing room. Of all the stubborn people in the world, Lucy Whitfield is the stubbornest. The queen of the mule-headed. Queen Elsie — no, Elsie was a cow. Queen Francis! That's it. Queen Francis the Talking Mule.

If only Lucy hadn't been named after Aunt Lucinda, then maybe she wouldn't feel like she had to pay attention to the old woman's words of warning. Of course it didn't help that Lucinda had been right about other things, terrible things. She'd predicted their mother's death, and done it at their father's funeral! "Five years," Aunt Lucinda had whispered to Lucy and Amanda as they watched their mother drop a handful of dirt onto their father's casket. "That's all she has left." Amanda had despised her for it — despised her at the time for making the prediction and despised her five years later for being right.

Aunt Lucinda's final prediction had been at their mother's deathbed. Hannah, her body wasted by cancer, had summoned the last of her strength to call Lucy to her side. Amanda and Aunt Lucinda had taken a few steps back as Lucy sat on the stool next to the bed. "Promise me you won't marry until after Amanda does," Hannah had rasped into Lucy's ear. "I know you're older, but Amanda needs someone to take care of her."

"I'll be fine, Mama," Amanda said over Lucy's shoulder. "Please don't worry about me."

Lucy turned and shushed her, then looked at her mother. "I promise, Mama. I'll wait until Amanda marries."

"If you don't, Amanda will die," Aunt Lucinda pronounced in a loud voice. "Gone a week after you take your vows."

"Oh, Cindy, don't say such a thing," Hannah had wheezed from her pillow. "It can't be true."

"I don't say things if they're not true," Aunt Lucinda said, pulling herself to her full height of five feet one inch. "If Lucy marries before Amanda, Amanda will die."

"Please don't worry, Mama," Lucy said as Hannah's eyes fluttered and then closed. "You have my word."

"I should hope so," Lucinda said. "She's your mother, after all."

"I know who she is," Lucy hissed at her aunt. "You don't have to tell me."

Aunt Lucinda is the worst person on the face of the earth, Amanda remembers thinking, and although Lucinda died only a few months after Hannah, and that was six years ago, Amanda thinks it still.

At the time of Lucinda's warning, Amanda assumed getting married in a timely fashion would present no problem at all. She was twenty-four, by all accounts pretty (if a little plump), and had had scores of boyfriends from seventh grade on. Nobody serious, although she longed for a deep, romantic love. An artist might do the trick, she'd thought in college, or a poet. But for reasons she could never understand, the artists weren't drawn to her and the poets left her alone, even when she was the only one who came to their readings. On the other hand, lacrosse players and political science majors rang her phone off the hook. But Amanda found them dull. They bought her beer when she longed for champagne, and not one of them dreamed of going to Paris or stealing kisses on top of the Empire State Building.

When she moved back home to help care for her mother, Amanda set her sights lower. Milton Falls was not known for its bohemian scene or literary salons. It was a scenic little river town with two inns and a proliferation of fall foliage that drew in the tourists from the end of September through mid-November. Young people left Milton Falls in droves after high school graduation and then returned in their middle years to raise their children on its neatly laid-out blocks, the schools all within walking distance of the neighborhoods they served. Unmarried men Amanda's age were few and far between. There had been that pleasant young school librarian, Joe Stillwell, who'd had such clean fingernails and a silver ring in his ear. If only he hadn't smelled of library paste and peanut butter! If only he hadn't constantly quoted his favorite lines from *Napoleon Dynamite.*

"You're too picky," Lucy always said, and Amanda supposed she was right. Joe Stillwell wasn't the only man Amanda had rejected. Jason Boyd, for instance, had been perfectly nice, and he was the assistant city manager, so he knew lots of good gossip about the mayor and the members of the city council. Emily had squeaked like a mouse when she'd heard he'd asked Amanda out. "He's a catch, Ammie!" she'd declared. "Remember how we all had crushes on him in high school?"

But Jason Boyd was a fingernail-biter and a spitter. On their first and only date, they took a walk down to the river, and he'd spit every five feet. How could Amanda spend the rest of her life with a man so full of saliva?

After Jason came Andrew Cross, who had a thriving law practice, but chewed with his mouth open and said "ek-specially" instead of "especially." Then there was Martin Grangerfield, who sold insurance and was always reciting statistics about activities that were likely to result in "personal mortality." That was his phrase, "personal mortality," and after he'd used it three times in ten minutes on their third and final date, Amanda feigned a fainting spell just to make him stop.

Now, at age thirty, Amanda has more or less given up. "It's you and me, Gretel," she's said to her cat more than once, and she says it now, walking into her sewing room and flipping on the light switch. She spent the last two days reorganizing, pressing and folding fabric, rounding up scissors and rulers and returning them to their proper places, tucking books back into bookshelves and poking pins into pincushions. At this very moment, her sewing room is not just her sewing room, it's her exact idea of what a sewing room should look like, a combination of artist's garret and fabric shop — swept hardwood floors and one wall almost entirely made of windows, panes sparkling after a good polishing, a sewing machine on a long table mirrored in the glass. Another wall is home to a six-by-six foot design wall and a cabinet of cubbies bursting with brightly patterned stacks of fabric. In the middle of it all sits an island with surfaces for cutting and ironing.

A marriage of true minds, Amanda thinks as she looks around the room, because she believes rooms do have minds. She believes that rooms — some rooms — are *enspirited*. They have feelings about the people who occupy them. Amanda believes her sewing room loves her as much as she loves it.

Stacked in the middle of the island is a tower of fabric sent to her from Paris by Aunt Tilly, the youngest of her mother's sisters, the one who said to Amanda when she was very young, "Don't think of me as your aunt; think of me as your fairy godmother." Aunt Tilly always sent the best presents from her apartment in the 3rd arrondissement, fairy wands and princess tiaras, hand puppets with reddened cheeks and silly noses, dolls that wore expressions of perfect sympathy and understanding. When Amanda turned twenty-one, Aunt Tilly sent fabric from Sophie Hallette, the most divine fabric shop in the world, she'd explained in her note. *You mustn't sew dresses with this, though you might well be tempted. Use it to make art. Use it to make quilts. You will be surprised by the results.*

Amanda had never thought of herself as an artist — she had made dresses for years, beautiful dresses, but she didn't consider them art — yet as soon as she held the beautiful linens and toiles in her hands, she knew exactly what to do. She hadn't felt the least twinge of fear before cutting into the fabric and then sewing the pieces into constellations of stars. It was as though the fabric had known from the beginning what it wanted to be and had simply guided Amanda's hands to make it so.

She'd gone on to make dozens of quilts over the years, most of them perfectly ordinary. But the quilts made from fabric sent by Aunt Tilly were special, and Amanda chose their recipients carefully. Toward the end of Hannah's illness, when she'd had trouble sleeping, Tilly sent Amanda a package filled with ocean green and pearl gray silks. Covered with the quilt Amanda had composed from the elegant yardage, Hannah's eyes grew heavy, her breathing deep. She slept.

The quilt she'd sewn for Vonnie was made from lustrous purple and teal batiks that Tilly had purchased at Brin de Cousette on rue Richard Lenoir. The first day Vonnie had lain beneath it, her nausea dissipated, never to return. By the third day, her hair began growing back and before long Vonnie could pull it into a ponytail.

The fabric that sits on the island is so gorgeous Amanda almost can't bring herself to touch it. She's afraid if she gets too close, she'll end up draping herself with the gold and persimmon prints, the luscious pumpkin yardage, and then run outdoors to traipse beneath the rising moon, much to the consternation of the neighbors. Tilly sent it more than two weeks ago, and Amanda has been waiting for the feeling, the one that tells her who the quilt will be for and how to start. She can't rush the feeling, can't force a revelation. All she can do is circle the fabric slowly several times a day, hold her hands over it, and occasionally caress it — if it doesn't feel too dangerous to do so.

Amanda sits on a stool across from the fabric and stares at it. *Tell me what to do*, she thinks, certain that the fabric can read her mind. Her hands so badly want to be buried in the folds, want to shake out each piece, lovingly run an iron over it. Will she use scissors or a rotary blade to cut it? Only the fabric knows what it wants. Only the fabric can tell her.

She is on the verge of giving up and heading back to the kitchen to steal some chocolate from Lucy's secret stash when a flash of light forces her head back. On the ceiling, she sees it. A quilt made of twelve wheels, each wheel cut into twelve wedges, each wedge like a ray of light shining out from the center. When done, the quilt will be luminous, a moon for any room it lives in.

The quilt will be for Lucy, Amanda suddenly realizes. It is what will allow Lucy — finally, finally — to give herself over to love.

She begins to cut right away — with scissors, it turns out, so that the circles are imperfect, which makes each one unique. Each circle will carry its own light, pour it out onto the world as it sees fit.

As always, Amanda works in a fever dream, the world

outside the windows falling away, day slipping into night, night's dark deepening and then lifting with the early morning birdsong. Amanda takes naps in a nest of quilts, steals to the kitchen for bread and apples and hurries back to her sewing room, not wanting the spell to be broken by talk. She keeps the radio tuned to the classical station where no one ever speaks, as though all its employees have taken a vow of silence.

At the end of the second day, the top is nearly finished. This is the point where Amanda begins to consider the quilting, what designs will work best, where the shapes and lines will shift and evolve and then return to themselves. She is tired now, and knows better than to keep sewing. She will drink tea, ponder, make sketches, sleep.

The moon is shining brightly through the kitchen window, no need for Amanda to turn on the light. As she fills the teakettle, she thinks about Lucy and how this quilt will change her. Amanda believes her sister is already in love with John Freeman; love is not the issue here. It's Lucy *allowing* herself to be in love, allowing herself to be open and vulnerable, to get past superstition and fear.

Amanda has a moment of panic. What if it's too late? What if John Freeman has given up, found someone else to be in love with? She hurriedly puts the kettle on the stove and turns the flame on high. She'll make orange pekoe instead of peppermint, get a bump of caffeine in her blood, and finish the quilt top before sunrise. After that, a little sleep, and then the quilting. If she works through this night and the next, the quilt will be done by Friday. Lucy can sleep beneath it, and in the morning, when she sees John at the farmers market, love will take its course.

Hurrying back to her studio, Amanda imagines what she'll wear as Lucy's maid of honor. Something shimmery and periwinkle, she decides. She will be the background against which Lucy shines. She wonders if Aunt Tilly will come from Paris for the wedding. Just imagine how much fabric she could carry in her suitcase, Amanda thinks as she lifts up the quilt top and slips it over her shoulders. Just imagine all the quilts it would make for Lucy's babies…

What wakes her first — the smell of smoke or the shriek of an alarm? Or is it the sensation of being lifted as though she were once again a small child, her father carrying her out to the backyard to see the lunar eclipse?

"We'll have you out of here in no time, ma'am," a man's voice says, and Amanda opens her eyes. She is in the arms of someone she's never seen before. He's dressed like a firefighter, and it takes Amanda a moment to realize he *is* a firefighter, complete with a yellow helmet with a badge that declares "Firefighter," in case there's any question.

The alarm seems to have risen an octave in its insistence that something is wrong. How could Amanda have slept through it? Usually the tiniest sounds wake her. *I must be exhausted*, she thinks, and rests her head against this stranger's shoulder.

"Your sister and your cat are already outside," the fireman says, and Amanda lifts her head again. Lucy and Gretel! She feels a retroactive wave of alarm surging through her. Who else needs saving? What else is in danger?

Lucy's quilt.

Amanda tries to scramble out of the fireman's arms. "I have to go back and get the quilt!" she says, pushing against the man's chest. His grasp is strong, though, and she gets nowhere.

"Would that be the quilt you're wearing, ma'am?" the fireman asks as they reach the front door. "Because that's the only one you're saving."

Amanda looks down. The unfinished quilt top is still wrapped around her shoulders. "Oh, thank goodness!" she sighs. And then she looks up into the fireman's face. His cheekbones are high, his nose large and slightly crooked. He has the kindest brown eyes she has ever seen. "Do I know you?" she asks, not sure what she hopes the answer will be.

"You do now," the fireman says with a smile.

"I guess I do," Amanda replies.

His name, Amanda learns the next day, is Wesley Bell. He has come back to check on the house, to make sure that the fire is completely out. "Things spark up where you least expect them," he explains as he pokes through the debris of the kitchen. "You think the fire has been extinguished, but it's just waiting for you to turn your back."

The kitchen is where most of the harm was done. Smoke has stained the walls throughout the house, and there is significant water damage in the front parlor. But the house itself has survived what Lucy is referring to as their tempest in a teapot. The kettle that started it all sits on the blackened stovetop, charred almost beyond recognition.

"I'm afraid the fire was my fault," Amanda feels the need to confess to Wesley Bell. "I was working on a quilt and needed a cup of tea. Only I fell asleep before the water boiled."

She knows she should be embarrassed or feel terrible, but in fact Amanda is giddy. She's so happy to have a reason to talk with Wesley Bell that she thinks she might set something on fire every day, just so he'll have to come over.

"A lot of fires start that way," Wesley says. "Midnight snacks. Grilled cheese sandwiches have started more fires in this county than lit cigarettes. Of course, that's mostly because people don't smoke much anymore."

"I love grilled cheese sandwiches," Amanda says. "With bacon. And sweet potato fries."

Wesley Bell smiles. His teeth, Amanda notes, are perfectly straight, except for left lateral incisor, which overlaps the front tooth in a way that Amanda finds adorable.

"I just got into sweet potato fries a couple of months ago," he says, leaning back against the counter. "Now it's like I have to have them every other day." He holds out his arm. "Do I look like I'm turning orange to you?"

"Maybe a little bit," Amanda says. Is she flirting? She's pretty sure she is, and she's pretty sure he is, and now they look at each other and smile, like they don't even have to talk if they don't want to. They're happy just to be in the same room.

"Wes! Let's head out," a voice calls from the front hall. "We have twenty pages of paperwork to fill out before lunch."

Wesley Bell straightens up, looks official and serious again. "I'll check in this afternoon," he says. "In the meantime, call us if you smell or see smoke."

"I will," Amanda says, following him out of the kitchen. "I promise."

The quilt top is draped over the newel post at the bottom of the stairs. Amanda doesn't remember hanging it there. Has Lucy brought it downstairs to air it out? How odd! Lucy treats Amanda's sewing space as sacrosanct. She never enters unless invited.

"Good luck getting the smell of smoke out of that," Wesley Bell tells Amanda. "Sometimes putting stuff in a bag with dryer sheets for a few hours works."

Amanda lifts the quilt top to her nose. "It doesn't smell like smoke at all," she says. "Isn't that odd?"

"That's really weird," Wesley Bell says. He leans over the quilt and sniffs. "It smells like cinnamon. It's nice — I mean it's a nice quilt. I always liked those colors."

"Pumpkin?" Amanda asks.

"And persimmon," Wesley Bell says. He glances at the quilt top again, and then looks back at Amanda. "Do you make a lot of quilts? Because I had the weirdest dream the other night — I was covered up in quilts, but it wasn't like I was smothering. It felt — well, it felt like being in love."

His face reddens at this admission, but he doesn't look away.

"I make a lot of quilts," Amanda says. "And I give most of them of them away, which makes this quilt unusual."

"How so?" Wesley Bell asks.

"Because," she says, suddenly realizing that she's known it all along, "this quilt is for me."

"Wes!" The voice from outside is insistent, and Wesley Bell shoves his Milton Falls Fire Department cap on his head and nods.

"I'll be back this afternoon," he tells Amanda. "You'll be here, right?"

"I'll be here," Amanda says. She watches Wesley Bell run down the sidewalk and hop into the truck. He leans over and punches his partner on the shoulder, grinning like he just won a big prize.

Lucy comes up and puts her arm around Amanda. "So, do you think everything is okay?" she asks. "I mean, with the house?"

Amanda takes her sister's hand. "I don't think we have anything to worry about," she says. "I think we're safe now."

Margaret Goes Modern

It's the show quilts that bore her the most during show-and-tell, all those elaborate medallions, all those persnickety Mariner's Compasses and their perfect points. Pointless points, Margaret thinks, perfectly pointless points. And the dreary colors, as though the competition quilters don't want beauty to detract from their technical accomplishments. *Bring on the mustards, bring on the browns and muted greens! Let me depress you with my palette.*

"You're awfully fidgety tonight," Ruth Starnes whispers from the next seat over. Up front, a show-and-teller is unscrolling her quilt with the help of two assistants. "Didn't you like the program?"

"It was fine," Margaret tells her, though now she can't remember what the program was. Oh, the group that makes quilts for dog shelters. What had they called themselves? The Grateful Threads? She'd almost raised her hand to inform them that she'd seen Jerry Garcia in a San Francisco coffee shop in 1968, and he'd not only been high as a kite, but he'd also poured out the contents of at least a dozen sugar packets on his table, clearly finding it hilarious, and then left two pennies in his coffee cup for a tip. Not exactly a man Margaret would name *her* charity group after. She leans over to Ruth and whispers, "Do you think dogs really want quilts? Don't you think they'd prefer pillows? Or maybe beanbag chairs?"

Ruth shushes her. "I want to hear what Gloria is saying," she says, pointing to the front of the fellowship hall, where Gloria Reynolds is holding up a quilt appliquéd with flower pots — red flowers, blue pots, lots of green vines snaking around the perimeter. It's nice, Margaret supposes, if you like that sort of thing. She used to like that sort of thing very much, but lately the appliqué patterns she sees in the magazines irritate her, all the pumpkins and sunflowers and little girls in sunbonnets. She wants to call up their designers and ask them what kind of dream world they're living in.

Okay, Margaret thinks, I'm done. She reaches down beneath her chair to grab her purse. It was a gift from her oldest daughter, Susan — expensive, leather, lots of buckles. "I'm going," she tells Ruth *sotto voce*. "I'm supposed to Skype with Maggie at eight forty-five, and I don't want to be late."

"How does she like William and Mary?" Ruth asks, handing Margaret her umbrella.

"Loves William, is so-so about Mary," Margaret says, and with that she makes her way down to the end of the row — *excuse me, excuse me, sorry about that* — and then heads toward the exit. It's Wednesday night and the church fellowship hall smells like burnt coffee. You'd suppose they'd be able to do something about that, Margaret thinks, but she's seventy-five, the veteran of a half dozen churches and three quilting guilds, and no matter what, the fellowship halls always smell like someone burned the coffee.

The Skype ringtone sounds a few times, a muted, flattened ring, as though it's underwater, and then suddenly Maggie appears on screen. Maggie is Margaret's eldest granddaughter and one of her handful of reasons for getting up each morning. Margaret doesn't recall Maggie's father or his sisters delighting her the way this eighteen-year-old girl does, but then, who has time to be delighted by her own children? There are moments, of course, mostly when they're sleeping, but the waking hours are so overlaid with busyness and worry that delight gets pushed out of the picture.

"Hi, Grammy," Maggie chirps. "It's great to see you!"

"Hello, my darling," Margaret says. "You look marvelous."

"I just got back from yoga. I'm so relaxed, I'm afraid I'm going to fall asleep as soon as I start studying."

The conversation continues the way their weekly conversations typically do, with Maggie doing most of the talking and Margaret doing most of the adoring. This girl, her namesake, is the reward for all the years of diaper changes and afterschool chauffeuring, for getting through Glenn's weekly speech therapy sessions, Susan's orthodontia and Ginny's punk rock years. Margaret loves her other grandchildren, of course, but Maggie was the first, and she was the only for five years, and she's the sweet-natured girl that neither of Margaret's daughters ever were.

"So Grammy, guess what?" Maggie asks, her blue eyes wide, her voice still girlish even though she's a college freshman now. "This girl on my hall has the coolest quilt her mom got her at Pottery Barn, and I was bragging that my grandmother made quilts, and she was like, 'that's so cool, you ought to get her to make you one for your bed!' And I remembered that you said you would, but I didn't know what the style would be like here, so I wanted to wait, but now I'm thinking maybe you could make me one?"

"You know I'm dying to make you a quilt for your dorm room," Margaret says. "What colors do you want?"

"Can I just show you the quilt?" Maggie asks, disappearing from the screen so that Margaret is left with a view of cinderblock walls and a poster that reads *Keep Calm and Eat Chocolate*. "She let me take it off her bed so you could see it."

"Of course, darling. Now, you'll have to let me know if it's the colors you like or the pattern..."

"Kind of both," Maggie says, her voice muffled. Suddenly the computer screen is filled with—well, something. Margaret can't quite make it out. A quilt, obviously, but what kind?

"Do you think you could stand back a little bit?" she asks. "So I can get the full view?"

"Sure, Grammy," Maggie says from behind the quilt. "Let me just move a few things out of the way."

As Maggie backs up, the quilt comes into focus. The only way Margaret can describe the pattern to herself is *off-balance*—four rows of squares-within-squares, white, teal, orange and fuchsia, each set of squares placed at a slightly different angle from the others, three per row, though *row* isn't actually the right word, as the squares aren't in a straight line. Strictly speaking, they're not (as far as Margaret can tell) blocks, but shapes set into the background fabric.

"That's the kind of quilt you want me to make you?" Margaret asks her granddaughter. "With that charcoal background, and the oranges and pinks?"

Maggie puts the quilt down and comes back to her computer. "And don't forget the teal," she says. "Do you like it? I just think it's so cool looking. It reminds me of modern art."

"I love it," Margaret says, although she's not sure that she does. "I'll see if I can find a picture of the design online and get started on it first thing in the morning."

"Oh, Grammy, thank you!" Maggie claps her hands. "You're the best!"

Margaret shrugs. "Anything for you, sweetie. Does your roommate want one too?"

"She's not here right now, but I'll ask her when she gets back," Maggie says. "That would be amazing to have matching beds!" And then her exuberant expression sobers into one of concern. "How's Gramps today? Is he doing okay?"

"Last I checked, he was in his study, doing his math problems," Margaret reports. "I should probably go look in on him again, remind him it's almost bedtime."

"Tell him I love him, okay? Remind him of that time we went to the zoo and I got so scared of the monkeys. I think he really likes that story."

Such a good girl, Margaret thinks after they've said their goodbyes. The minute Maggie turned thirteen, Margaret had worried and waited — for the piercings, the tattoos, the foul language, the alcohol and drugs. But somehow

Maggie had managed to avoid the uglier side of teen culture. Really, Margaret thinks, someone should give Glenn and Denise a medal.

She rises from her computer, supposing she should go ahead and check on James, although she knows he'll be exactly where she left him before she sat down in the kitchen to Skype, in his study, at the architect's table he uses for a desk, his calculus textbook in front of him. The last time Margaret checked he was going over chapter 8 again, "Exponential and Logarithmic Functions."

"Is it any easier this time around?" she'd asked him, and he replied, "A little easier this time. I think I'm improving."

What he means is, he thinks his brain is improving. He thinks he can fight Alzheimer's with math. Since his diagnosis this past spring, James has tackled algebra, geometry and trigonometry. A retired history teacher, he believes that studying math will open up new circuits in his brain, plow through plaque deposits and straighten out tangled wires.

It could work, Margaret tells the children, who call more frequently since James' diagnosis — particularly Ginny, whose guilt at being a problem child for so many years rises up to the surface of every conversation. "You're nice now," Margaret tells her, "that's all that matters." But it's not enough for her youngest daughter, who sometimes calls as many as three times a week, to Margaret's annoyance. Really, how much is there to say? What she says to all of the children is: "Maybe your dad's plan will work; he seems fine — a little forgetful, but fine."

But she knows the math is not working, and neither is the exercise or the dairy-free diet. Just yesterday she'd found James holding a picture of his sister. "She's a pleasant-looking woman," he said. "Friend of yours?"

Margaret pads down the hallway to the study, thinking about the quilt Maggie wants her to make. Is there a pattern for that sort of thing? Maybe she should go to Thimble Pleasures in the morning and talk to Julie, who's so knowledgeable about quilt patterns. If Margaret can find a picture to show her, she's sure the two of them can figure it out. But she'd rather have directions to tell her what to do.

The door to James' study is cracked open, allowing a wedge of light to escape into the dark hallway. "Maybe it's time to call it a night, sweetheart," Margaret says as she goes in. "It's getting late."

James holds up a hand to signal that he's in the middle of a problem. He's like a boy getting ready for a big test in the morning, Margaret thinks, and then shakes her head in irritation. Stop it, she tells herself. She can't afford to get sentimental or maudlin. Ginny can wail and beat her chest; Margaret has to concern herself with the long run.

A moment later, James shuts his textbook and turns around. "I'll wait until the morning to check my answers," he says. "But I think I've finally got this stuff mastered. It's like learning a second language, you know? A new alphabet."

"You should take up quilting," Margaret says. "You'd get the math and the movement at the same time. It's like a workout, making a quilt."

"Maybe when I finish calculus — or, no, after that I'm going to do linear algebra. I have no idea what that is, do you?"

"Never heard of it," Margaret says. "But I'm sure it's interesting."

"It's funny how I never liked math much as a student," James says, pushing himself up from his chair. "But now I think I get it—I mean, in a more philosophical way. A deeper way. I was thinking that for Christmas, one of the children could give me a Great Courses DVD on Einstein."

"I'll mention it to Glenn the next time I talk to him," Margaret says, taking James' arm and guiding him toward the door.

James looks at her, clearly confused. "Glenn?"

Margaret doesn't let herself react; she takes a deep breath instead. She has read about what to do when your spouse forgets important people in his life. Reframe. Provide a historical reference. Don't make a big deal out of it.

"Yes, I think Glenn would enjoy giving you that," she says. "Do you remember when he took physics in high school? Of all our children, he'd been the least interested in science, and suddenly he thought he was going to be an astronaut."

James smiles, though there is a hint of panic in his eyes. He remembers who Glenn is now, but he's clearly alarmed that he forgot, if only for a moment.

Margaret squeezes her husband's arm. "Who knew he'd be a doctor instead? And a foot doctor at that?"

"He always did like shoes," James says, and Margaret smiles. It is their old joke. She hopes their jokes are the last thing to go.

II.

"You're going modern on me!" Julie says the next morning as she looks at the pictures Margaret has printed out from the Internet. "Most of the quilters who come in wanting to make a modern quilt are under forty."

Margaret raises an eyebrow. "And you're saying I'm not?"

"Sorry, it's just that everyone I know under forty has at least three visible tattoos, and I don't see any ink on you."

"And you never will," Margaret says, following Julie toward a wall of solids. "Can you imagine, at my age?"

"What, thirty-nine?"

"Exactly."

Margaret has never used many solids in her quilts, and standing in front of the wide array of fabric now, she's surprised by the number of incremental variations within each colorway, even the whites, of which there are five. "Which pink do you think is the right pink?" she asks. "The raspberry or the hot pink?"

"I'd go with the hot pink," Julie says, pulling out the bolt from the wall. "The brighter the better, especially if you're going to use a darker gray for the background. At the guild meeting, you see a lot of intense color. A lot of really shocking fuchsias."

"At the Elizabeth County Quilters guild meeting?" Margaret can't think of the last time she's been shocked by color at a meeting. There are a few quilters who are ambitious in their use of batiks, but she can't think of when anyone's use of pink has surprised her, much less caused her alarm.

"No, no — the Modern Quilt Guild meeting. They meet here every third Sunday — this coming Sunday as a matter of fact. You should come, now that you're into modern quilts. Seriously, the meetings are a lot of fun. It's a different sort of group." Julie pauses to smile. "Lots of ink."

After they pull the fabric, they sit down at Julie's computer to work out the measurements so they'll know how much to cut from each bolt. "Now you get the idea of these squares within squares, right?" Julie asks. "You start with a square — well, it's not really a square, is it? Let's call it a wonky square. And then you sew a strip to each side — "

"Also wonky?" Margaret asks. The word feels strange in her mouth. What was that movie? Oh, *Willy Wonka*. It had been Ginny's favorite, but Margaret had found it stressful. She'd been so sure someone was going to fall into that chocolate river, and she'd been right.

"No, but of different widths. And easy as pie, you've got your square within a square. And then you have to set it in the gray fabric… "

Julie goes on to explain how to construct the rest of the quilt, and Margaret realizes it won't take more than an afternoon or two to finish the top. And then she'll have to make a second one for Maggie's roommate. She wonders if her longarmer, Kate, has some space next week. In the pictures, the quilting is all straight lines. Nothing to it.

"I suppose I could quilt it myself," she says out loud. "It seems fairly simple."

"Come to the meeting on Sunday," Julie says. "One of the members is talking about how to quilt a modern quilt. It can be a fairly straightforward process, but there are some tricks. Besides, I think you'd like the group."

Walking out to her car with her bag of fabric and thread, Margaret wonders if that's true. She supposes it might do her some good to spend time with young people. Her life is filled with old people — old people at her guild meeting, old people at church, old people in the doctor's office — and it has its fair share of middle-aged people as well. Nowadays when her children call, they lament about their failing eyes, their upcoming colonoscopies, their knees. They're shocked by the decline of their bodies. Susan in particular feels betrayed. Like every pretty woman Margaret has ever known, Susan thought the gods of aging would pass over her, leaving her unscathed. Sometimes when she's listening to Susan talk about the bags under her eyes or her sagging neck, Margaret goes into the bathroom and looks at herself in the mirror. Her face is a collection of lines, a map of brown spots. *But at least I've got my own teeth*, she always thinks, and then Susan asks, "Mom, why are you laughing?"

The problem with going to the Modern Quilt Guild meeting is that she'll have to leave James alone at dinner, and there's something about that idea that unnerves Margaret. It's not that she's afraid he'll forget the stove is on and burn down the house; it's more the image of him eating by himself in front of the TV that makes Margaret hesitate. She imagines the television's glow reflected in his glasses, his mouth going slack between bites as he absorbs the action on the screen, and she can't help but think of her mother in the nursing home, sitting in a wheelchair as she ate lunch and watched soap operas, her chin speckled with spaghetti sauce.

So when Ginny calls after lunch on Sunday to say she's going to come by later with the kids and will pick up something from Boston Market for dinner, Margaret asks if she would mind staying until seven-thirty so she can attend the meeting. "Of course," Ginny assures her. "The kids would love to have extra time with Gramps."

Margaret still marvels at her youngest child's willingness to please. Of course, Ginny is forty-five now, married for fifteen years, and has been a dutiful daughter since her own daughter was born ten years ago. The scales fell from her eyes, James liked to joke, and verily, it seemed as though they had. Well, nobody knew how hard it was to be a parent until they became one. And at least Ginny has the grace to admit how difficult she'd been and is doing her best to make up for it. Sometimes it's true that Margaret would like to make the sign of the cross over her daughter's head and say: "You are absolved of all wrong-doing, stop apologizing." She wonders if Ginny has more to feel guilty about than Margaret realizes.

The minivan pulls into the driveway at four-thirty. When the back door slides open the children bound out. "Mom said it takes ninety minutes to get here, but she was wrong!" Cameron yells to Margaret, who's waiting on the front porch. "It took ninety-five minutes and forty-seven seconds. I timed it!"

Ginny, eyes on her phone, is slower out of the car. "Grammy can hear you, Cam; turn the volume way down." She presses a button on her keychain and the van's hatch lifts open. "Do you have time to eat before you go, Mom? This food smells amazing."

"I'll eat when I get back," Margaret tells her. She turns

to Jenna, who is staring up into the branches of an oak tree. "What do you see up there, sweetie?"

"I thought I saw a raven," Jenna says. "Which I think is a sign? There's a book I'm reading where if a raven shows up in a dream, it means something's going to happen. I think that the raven in the tree means that Gramps is going to get better."

Margaret puts an arm around the girl and hugs her close. Nearly ten, Jenna is bookish and dreamy. In a recent phone conversation, she declared her belief that Hogwarts was a real place and that she was waiting for her letter of acceptance. "I think the Sorting Hat would put me in Hufflepuff," she said, sounding disappointed, but resigned. "Oh, you might be surprised," Margaret had assured her. "You might find yourself in Gryffindor yet."

"Kids, why don't you run inside and find Gramps? Ask him if he wants to eat now or wait until later." Ginny walks up to the porch, a bulging plastic bag in either hand. "You should eat, Mom. There's chicken and potato salad — I'd be happy to fix you a plate."

Margaret waves off the offer. "I'm not hungry. I'll get something later."

"You doing okay?" Ginny asks, her voice gentle, sympathetic. "You sounded a little tired on the phone earlier. Do you think it's time to hire someone?"

"Hire someone? For what?" Margaret asks, as though she doesn't know.

"To help with Dad, give you a little break."

"But I don't need help with Dad. Your father doesn't need help, period. He's fine. It could be years before we need anything like that."

Margaret opens the screen door and gestures for Ginny to go inside. "Really, Ginny, don't worry so much. There'll be a time for worrying and bringing in nurses, but we're not there yet."

"Is it possible you're in denial, Mom?" Ginny asks as she walks into the kitchen and drops the bags of food on the counter. "You're a tough customer, we all know that, but sooner or later you're going to have to admit that Dad is sick."

Margaret resists the urge to say something sarcastic like, *Not as sick as I am of this conversation*. She resists pulling up ancient history as a way of punishing Ginny for being a patronizing know-it-all. Instead, she says as calmly as she can, "I'm fully aware of your father's medical condition, Ginny. I take him to all of his appointments, I confer with his doctors, I track his medications. Believe me, I know what's going on, and when it's time to get a home health worker, I will do just that. But for now, we're fine. I'm fine."

"Okay, I get it," Ginny says in tone of voice that suggests she thinks Margaret is delusional but that perhaps it's best to change the topic. She reaches into one of the bags and pulls out a roll and a napkin. "At least eat a little. The meeting might go on longer than scheduled. You never know."

Margaret takes the roll and bites into it. It's yeasty and soft, the sort of thing she usually doesn't allow herself. But today she gives in, if only to do one thing that will make Ginny happy. "Delicious," she says, her mouth full. "Don't let Dad eat all of them before the kids get some."

III.

Driving to the meeting, she resists the temptation to open the bag on the passenger seat and peek inside. She's not sure why she's brought the quilt tops with her, other than she likes them and wants Julie to look at them and like them, too. As she suspected, the quilt tops didn't take long to make; Margaret had the second one finished by Saturday afternoon. What she didn't expect was that she would be so pleased with them. Such a simple design, but Margaret can't stop looking, she's so delighted by this pattern that isn't quite a pattern.

The meeting is being held in the classroom at Thimble Pleasures. The tables have been folded up and four rows of chairs have been set out. It's a few minutes after five when Margaret arrives, and most of the seats are taken. She finds a place to stand in the back, but Julie comes up behind her and guides her to a chair in the last row. "You don't want to be on your feet the entire time," Julie insists, and Margaret supposes she's right. Taking a seat, she pushes her bag under the chair and turns her attention to the front, where a young woman who doesn't appear to be much older than Maggie is making announcements. To Margaret's surprise, the woman in the seat next to her leans over and whispers: "Hi, I'm Erica. I haven't seen you here before." Her arms are completely covered with tattoos, some primitive, others complicated and complex. Without thinking, Margaret says, "That's a lot of ink."

Erica laughs. She has a broad face, pleasant, almost handsome, and short, dyed-black hair, shaved close on the sides. Holding out both arms, she nods. "Yeah, I've got a couple of sleeves here, don't I?"

Sleeves. Margaret considers this as they turn their attention back to the front of the room, where the young woman — the guild president, Margaret supposes — is now yielding the floor to a man who appears to be in his thirties, maybe even early forties. He's balding, which makes it difficult for Margaret to pinpoint his age. She wonders if under his jacket he, too, has a sleeve of tattoos. She's at a loss as to why people do that to themselves, treat their skin as if it were a piece of paper, a canvas. She glances at Erica's arms. They look like comic books, the kind that Glenn used to read, with dark lords and heroic underdogs, the settings vaguely medieval.

"Okay, as most of you know, I'm Steve, a.k.a. Quilt Guy," the man says as he connects a laptop to a projector. "Today we're going to talk about free motion quilting, with a focus on negative space. I decided to make a video, because I knew it would thrill you to see me actually sewing instead of just talking about sewing."

What follows is a five-minute video with Steve, a.k.a. Quilt Guy, pontificating from behind his sewing machine. "Negative space isn't just background space," he says to the camera. "It's whatever space isn't occupied by design, and the quilting there really stands out." He holds up an unquilted square and then puts it under the needle. Margaret sits mesmerized as he moves the square around ("Remember everyone, feed-dogs down!"), filling it with circles as small as dimes and as large as half dollars ("Vary your size for visual interest!"). He demonstrates on other quilt squares — spirals and squares, straight lines sewn close together and then farther apart.

When the video ends, Margaret turns to Erica and asks, "I wonder if Julie carries those gloves he was wearing, with the little bumps on them?"

"She usually does," Erica says. "And she also carries the Supreme Slider he was using. Have you ever tried that?"

Margaret shakes her head. "I've never done any of my own quilting. Well, I hand-quilted back when everyone did. But I've been quilting by check for at least twenty-five years. What's a supreme slider?"

"How about after the meeting, I show you everything you need to machine quilt?" Erica offers. "Julie lets us shop even though the store's closed."

"Oh, I don't want to trouble you," Margaret says. Suddenly she feels shy — she's not used to young women befriending her. Quite the opposite, really. Ginny hardly spoke to her for most of her twenties, and Susan was so busy working as an associate in a law firm that her weekly phone calls home never lasted more than ten minutes.

"It's no trouble!" Erica insists. "I love getting people addicted to machine quilting. You'll thank me later."

"Well, if you're sure," Margaret says. And then, because she can't help herself, she asks, "What does your mother think of your tattoos?"

"She was especially fond of this one." Erica points to the tattoo that takes up most of her left forearm — a woman warrior with a gold breastplate and a fierce expression. "After all, it's her."

"That's your mother?"

Erica nods. "She died last year of breast cancer. We thought she was going to kick cancer's butt, and she almost did. I got this tattoo as a way of encouraging her. Up to that point, she hated all of my tattoos. But this one she loved."

"My daughter Ginny has a tattoo on her hip," Margaret confides as Steve packs up his laptop and projector and the guild president returns to the lectern. "A tiger. She doesn't know I know. Her sister told me."

"Do you mind?" Erica asks. "I mean, that your daughter has a tattoo?"

Margaret considers this. "I used to. I don't understand why people get tattoos, really. But now I think what I really mind is that she never told me. I don't know why she would — she knows I wouldn't like it — but I wish we had that sort of relationship. The sort where you tell each other the truth about yourselves."

"That's a hard sort of relationship to come by," Erica says. The guild president has started to talk again, and Erica lowers her voice. "Especially between mothers and daughters. It took my mother dying for me to tell her the truth about anything. Well, she knew about the tattoos."

"How could she not?"

"Exactly," Erica whispers. "Some things you just can't hide."

The guild president clears her throat. "Okay, unless somebody has anything else we need to discuss, it's time for show-and-tell," she announces. "I really want to encourage newcomers to share if you've brought something — it's the best way I know to introduce yourself to the group. And we are an extremely appreciative audience."

Erica looks at Margaret expectantly. "Well? Are you going up? I know you've got something in that bag you shoved under your chair."

"And just how do you know that?" Margaret asks, stalling. She's a show-and-tell veteran, a woman used to appreciative applause and even the occasional gasp, but this is different. Just because she likes the quilt tops in her bag doesn't mean this crowd will. Maybe she's done modern all wrong.

"Have I misjudged?" Erica asks, one eyebrow raised. "Because I don't think I have."

When Margaret doesn't answer, Erica continues. "Come on! It's a great way to break the ice. Besides, I really want to see what you've made."

"Fine," Margaret says, pretending to be irritated, but secretly a little flattered by Erica's insistence. "But if I'm booed off the stage… "

"Honey, it's really not that kind of crowd," Erica says, raising her hand. "Sonia? We have a volunteer right here. This is — well, I don't actually know her name."

"Margaret Daniels," Margaret supplies, reaching under her chair to grab her bag. "I'm a quilter."

"Hi, Margaret!" the crowd responds in unison.

Margaret makes her way up to the front of the room. "I'm new to modern quilting, but not to quiltmaking. Still, if these are ridiculous, please let me know. I'm making them for my granddaughter."

Sonia, the guild president, takes the first top as Margaret pulls it from the bag, unfurling it for the group to see. There are *oohs* and *aahs*, and somebody claps spontaneously. "Love it," a voice calls out. "Great colors!"

"Julie helped me work out the pattern," Margaret says, directing her remarks to Erica, who is beaming at her from her seat. "My granddaughter, Maggie — she's a freshman at

William and Mary and smart as a whip — saw a bedspread from Pottery Barn and thought I could make something similar to it."

"That's a million times better than Pottery Barn," a woman in the second row says. "I find the Pottery Barn stuff depressing."

"Denyse Schmidt designed a quilt for Pottery Barn," someone points out. "*Single Girl*? It's a really cool quilt."

"It's a really cool *mass-produced* quilt," the first woman replies, and a wave of voices rises up as a number of people begin to spontaneously debate the point.

Margaret has no idea who this Denyse Schmidt person is, and now she's afraid she's committed some sort of faux pas by being inspired by a factory-made quilt. Is that not allowed in modern quilting?

"How do you plan on quilting it?" Erica calls, her voice breaking through the chatter. "Are you going to do it yourself?

Margaret smiles. Ah, the dependable friend who steers the conversation back from chaos to its original course. "I was hoping you'd tell me how," she says, and Erica gives her the thumbs up sign.

The rest the audience thinks she means she wants *them* to tell her how, and so the wave of voices rises again, this time with helpful suggestions for quilting patterns and thread choices. Margaret listens and nods, charmed by these young people who are doing their best to make her feel at home.

IV.

For the second time in a week, Margaret leaves Thimble Pleasures loaded down with new purchases. She has a LaPierre Studio Supreme Slider Free Motion Machine Quilting Mat, Fons and Porter Machine Quilting Grip Gloves, two books on free motion quilting by a woman she's never heard of named Angela Walters, and a darning foot for her Bernina.

"Do you drink?" Erica asked her while they were standing in front of the notions wall, and when Margaret replied that she had a glass of wine on occasion, Erica smiled. "Good. A glass of wine is your best friend when you're machine quilting. The key is to be as relaxed as possible while still being able to operate heavy machinery."

Then Erica called to a woman leafing through pattern books across the room. "Lauren, come meet Margaret! I'm converting her to machine quilting."

"Hold onto your wallet!" Lauren said as she crossed the room. When she reached them, she put her arm around Erica and pulled her close. "I think Julie has this one on commission."

"Margaret, I'd like you to meet my girlfriend, Lauren," Erica said, leaning into Lauren's embrace. "She exaggerates, but only slightly. Julie has been known to toss a couple of yards of Kona solids my way after a particularly good sale."

"I liked the quilt you showed today, Lauren," Margaret said, proud of herself for talking to the woman in a normal tone of voice, as though she met lesbians every day of the week. “I thought it was lovely.”

“Did you really?” Lauren asked. “I don’t know. It looked so good in my head, but in real life, I’m not sure it works.”

Margaret laid a reassuring hand on the young woman’s arm. “I’m new to modern quilting, but I’m not new to design or color, and I thought your quilt was quite striking.”

“I can’t believe those are your first modern quilts,” Lauren said, squeezing Margaret’s hand. “They’re great! Have you decided how you’re going to quilt them?”

“Erica has offered several ideas,” Margaret told her. Lauren rolled her eyes. “I’m sure she has,” she said. “Erica has lots of opinions.”

“All of them correct,” Erica added.

Thinking about the two women as she loads her bags into the backseat of her car, Margaret smiles. They are in their mid-twenties, both of them in graduate school for social work. Talking with them, Margaret was reminded what a wonderful, terrible thing it is to be a young adult, old enough to be out of your parents’ house and not tethered to marriage, mortgages or children, but still so young and insecure. She can still see Ginny when they’d picked her up from the airport one Christmas — she’d been twenty-three or twenty-four — walking into the waiting area in her leather jacket, raggedy flannel shirt and holey jeans over black tights, her short hair dyed red, those horrible black boots she wore every single day she was home, even when they went to church. She looked like someone who belonged in the cast of *Oliver Twist*. But she was so full of dreams — maybe she’d get a job writing television screenplays in Los Angeles, maybe she’d start a restaurant. “You are a marvelous mess,” James had said to her one night, and Ginny had laughed. "Emphasis on the *marvelous*, I'm sure," she'd said dryly.

Emphasis on the *mess*, Margaret remembers thinking.

Sighing, Margaret gets in the car and puts the key in the ignition. Maybe if she'd done a better job trying to understand who Ginny was in her late teens and early twenties — listened to some of the music she loved so much, read some of her favorite novels — she could have steered her in the right direction, away from the alcoholic musician boyfriends and bartending jobs of her post-college years. But no, Margaret hadn't taken Ginny's interests seriously, couldn't believe that Ginny took them seriously.

James tried to do those things, she remembers. He read the books, listened to the music. He called Ginny every Sunday afternoon, talked with whichever housemate answered the phone wherever Ginny was living — Seattle, Austin, Minneapolis — made jokes, tried to connect. And now Ginny was the one making the phone calls, trying to connect. If she ever got a tattoo on her forearm — and Margaret seriously hoped she wouldn't — it would be of her father, not her mother. James was the hero. Margaret was the one always saying no.

By the time Margaret gets home, it's almost eight o'clock. James and the children are watching a movie in the family room, Ginny is in the kitchen, on the computer.

"I thought you went to a meeting," she says when she sees Margaret with her bags. "It looks like you've been to the mall."

"Oh, you know how it is with quilting," Margaret tells her daughter, depositing the bags on the kitchen table.

"You can't walk out of the quilt shop without spending at least a hundred dollars."

"I thought that was Target," Ginny says, laughing. "Or at least that's always been *my* problem at Target. I went in last week to get a new laundry basket and came home with two rugs, three trashcans, a scented candle and a week's worth of groceries. The funny thing is, I forgot to get the laundry basket."

She stands. "Want me to make you a cup of tea before I go?"

"That would be lovely," Margaret says, taking a seat at the table. "My meeting was fun, but I think I'm worn out now."

"I'm so glad you're still quilting," Ginny says. She walks over to the stove and reaches for the kettle. "I think that's really important."

"Quilting has always been important to me," Margaret replies. "Why would that be different now?"

"I'm just saying, what with Dad being sick..."

Margaret, uninterested in pursuing this line of conversation, cuts her daughter off. "Do you remember that band you used to work for?" she asks. "What were they called? The Naked Pants?"

Ginny's eyes widen. "What in the world made you think of that?"

"I don't know," Margaret says with a shrug. "So was it the Naked Pants?"

"The Naked Trousers. I used to manage them, which just means I got them gigs in clubs around Austin. But really, what made you think of that?"

"Did you know your dad tracked down a CD they

made? This was in the days before iTunes, maybe even before the Internet, so he had to go to some hole-in-the-wall record store downtown and order it. One day I went back to his study, and there he was, listening to The Naked Trousers. When I asked him what he thought, he said, 'I don't know if I like it, but it's interesting.'"

Ginny carries the kettle to the sink to fill it. It's a moment before she speaks. "I didn't know he did that," she says in a ragged voice. "He never told me."

"You were always his favorite," Margaret says. "I mean, he loved all of you so much, but you were special."

Ginny looks out the kitchen window. "How can you stand it? How can you stand what's happening to him?"

"Nothing's happened yet," Margaret says. "At least not much has happened. I refuse to mourn him before he's gone."

Ginny turns and looks at her. "I want to help you, Mom."

"Then make me some tea. I'd like peppermint."

Ginny makes the tea and Margaret begins pulling everything from her bags, the gloves, the quilting mat, the books. "I met some very nice young women at the meeting tonight," she says, trying on one of the gloves. "They had tattoos. Well, Lauren only had a small tattoo on her wrist, but Erica had two sleeves."

Ginny sniffs, then laughs. "How do you even know what a sleeve is?" she asks, walking over to the table carrying two mugs of tea.

"I'm very modern these days," Margaret says. "Erica has a tattoo of her mother on her arm. Maybe I'll get a tattoo. A sewing machine or a needle and thread. What do you think?"

"I know a guy in Evansville, very clean shop," Ginny says. She sits down across the table from Margaret. "I have a tattoo, you know."

"I know. A tiger on your hip. Susan told me."

Ginny shakes her head. "She's such a fink."

They drink their tea without talking. Just as Ginny starts to push her chair away from the table, Cam walks into the kitchen, his face pale.

"Gramps keeps calling me Glenn," he reports. "Even after I told him a bunch of times that I'm Cam, not Glenn. It's starting to scare me."

"He knows who you are, honey. He's just tired," Ginny tells him, standing up. "Why don't you get your things and tell Jenna it's time to go."

When Cam leaves the room, Ginny turns and looks at Margaret.

"What?" Margaret asks, her voice defiant, but she can't hold Ginny's gaze. Instead she opens one of the machine quilting books and starts flipping through the pages. She sees a quilt that reminds her of Lauren's, and she wonders if Lauren and Erica are home by now, if they've poured themselves glasses of wine and are at work on new quilts.

What had she told Erica during the meeting — that she wished she and Ginny had the kind of relationship where they told each other the truth about themselves? Margaret's eyes blur with tears. How can she tell the truth when she's such a liar?

"Mom? Are you okay?"

Margaret nods, and then she shakes her head. No, she is not okay. She is a million miles away from okay.

"I'm scared," she whispers, staring straight ahead. "I'm

scared that one day your father will wake up and he won't know who I am."

Ginny comes and puts her hands on Margaret's shoulders. She leans down so that their cheeks are touching. "I like that quilt in your book," she says after a minute, her voice soft. "The one on the left-hand page."

"That one?" Margaret asks, pointing to a quilt made up of rows of stars — wonky stars, Julie would call them — hot pink stars against a dark blue sky.

"That's the one," Ginny says, sitting down next to her. "How hard would it be to make that one?"

"Not hard at all," Margaret says. "Do you want me to make it for you?"

"No, I mean, how hard would it be for *me* to make it?" Ginny's voice is gentle, and suddenly Margaret realizes her daughter is trying to give her a gift, has been trying to give her gifts for a long time now, only Margaret hasn't known how to receive them. She thinks of Erica's tattoo, her way of telling her mother *I love you.*

"Not hard at all," Margaret says, and for some reason she's blinking back tears again. "There's not much to it. I could help. Picking out the right colors would be the hardest thing. As Erica says, if you're going to keep it simple, you better make it beautiful."

"Erica's the one with the tattoos?"

"Yes, that's the one. You'd like her, I think. And not just because of the tattoos. She reminds me of you at that age."

Ginny looks suspicious. "In a good way or a bad way?"

Margaret looks at her daughter. For the first time, she notices the wrinkles fanning out from the corner of Ginny's eyes, the strands of gray in her hair. She reaches over and pats Ginny's hand. "Erica reminds me of you in a marvelous way, I'd say. Now, let's talk about this quilt you're going to make."

Improv

Liz glances at the picture on her computer screen one last time. A family in untucked white shirts and rolled-up khakis smiles back at her, the summer sunset illuminating their faces. They are, of course, barefoot. The man is tall and casually handsome with a vacation's worth of stubble shading his chin, the woman has shining blue eyes and perfectly windswept hair. She leans into her husband's shoulder while pulling her two young daughters — blonde like their mother, adorable like their mother — into her embrace. Someone has said something to make them all laugh, or perhaps they simply find themselves so delightful they can't help but let the joy spill out and encircle them like a wreath.

The caption reads: "Christmas Card photo reveal — I think! Haven't decided, but I love how this picture came out, don't you?" Liz knows she's supposed to comment *What a beautiful family!* like everyone else. And it's true — the Wrights are beautiful, individually and as a collective. But what she really wants to write is, *I bet Dan is cheating on you.* Which is a horrible, mean-spirited thing even to think of writing, not to mention a lie. She has no idea whether Dan cheats or not. It's just that the excess of perfection always makes her a little cranky.

Maybe it's time to unfriend Sherri Wright.

Liz positions the arrow over Sherri's name so that the options reveal themselves. She doesn't have to unfriend; she could unfollow instead and no one would be the wiser. But she likes the finality of unfriending. She likes how it would lock her out of Sherri's Facebook feed for good, take away the temptation to peek at it from time to time. Was Sherri running a marathon this weekend? Volunteering with her family at the food bank? Maybe she was spending Saturday night by the backyard fire pit and ruminating about the pleasures of giving her daughters a simple, old-fashioned childhood.

No devices for us! she'd posted a week ago, sharing a picture of Austen and MacKenzie at the kitchen table filling in complicated coloring books with colored pencils. Liz couldn't help comparing the technology-free Wright girls with her own daughter, Kate, who at the time was playing *The Daring Game for Girls* on her Nintendo DS while simultaneously watching *The Black Stallion* on her laptop for the nine-hundredth time.

Unfriend. Liz clicks and Sherri Wright is deleted from her life. Well, from her Facebook life anyway. They're still neighbors. Liz will still receive Sherri's text every morning, Monday through Friday, informing her that Kate has made it to the bus stop safely, and another one each afternoon to say that the bus has arrived and Kate is on her way home.

"You're so brave to let her walk by herself!" Sherri exclaimed with a shudder earlier in the fall when Liz had informed the other bus stop moms that she would no longer be walking Kate to the bus stop every morning or waiting for her at the end of the day. "I guess I'm just not ready to let go yet," Sherri said.

"It's five minutes from our house," Liz replied, barely tamping down her exasperation, "and she only has to cross one street. And she's ten. I walked half a mile to school every morning when I was ten. It was fine."

Sherri and the other bus stop moms all smiled and said, *Oh sure, of course*. But their expressions made it clear that they thought Liz was making a huge mistake, one that would likely result in Kate's face appearing on the six o'clock news some day. "I'll text you every morning when she gets here," Sherri promised, and when Liz said that wouldn't be necessary, she'd laughed. "Believe me, you'll want to know!"

Kate, who was sitting on the curb at the time and pretending to read *Origami Yoda*, looked up to glare at Sherri. "I don't need somebody to spy on me."

Sherri laughed as though she thought Kate was just too cute. "It takes a village, honey."

"To do what," Kate asked before turning back to her book, "totally violate a person's privacy?"

Sherri shot the other bus stop moms a quick, knowing glance that made Liz think Kate was a topic of discussion among them.

Enough. Liz gets up from the computer and goes into the kitchen to make tea. She spent all morning on her article about upcoming crafts fairs for the local magazine where she is less-than-gainfully employed as the one and only staff writer, and now she wants to work on her latest quilt until Kate gets home. *Not work*, she can hear her best friend and former college roommate Polly insist. *Remember, it's play!*

Easy for Polly to say. Polly lives in a loft in downtown Minneapolis and plays with fabric for a living. She is the quilt-o-sphere's most famous improvisational artist, cutting up old polyester shirts and table cloths, piecing them together in wild configurations, and then writing books and teaching classes about her process. Liz smiles as she takes out her rotary cutter and a ruler. Using a ruler is just one of many traditional processes her friend sniffs at. "You'll never make the quilt police happy," Polly likes to point out. "So why try?"

It is their ongoing, long-running argument. Polly has built a career on thumbing her nose at the so-called quilt police, that imaginary posse of tight-lipped ladies who are constantly judging quilts on the evenness of their stitches and the fullness of their bindings. Liz is no perfectionist herself, but sometimes rules are helpful. Not everyone can be an improvisational genius like Polly. Liz has tried Polly's methods, but the quilts she's made using Polly's book *No More Rules! No More Rulers!* never make her happy. They strike her as visually muddy, unlike the quilt she's working on now, her Modern Bear Claw, which practically makes her dance with its sharp demarcations and its surprisingly crisp blue and orange batiks. Batiks, as Liz is perfectly aware, are not strictly part of the modern aesthetic, but in this regard she's as unconcerned as Polly about rules.

She has finished the piecing and is plotting out her overall design, deciding how best to float her blocks across a white background, when her phone buzzes. Is it possible that two hours have passed? No, the time on the screen reads: 1:46. So why is Sherri texting her? She feels a jangle of nerves as she swipes to read the message. Given Sherri's near constant presence at the school as a parent volunteer, she'd be the first to know about an emergency — a crazed gunman in the cafeteria, a fire in the art room.

But the text begins *Hey Writer Girl*, and Liz lets out her breath. No bad news has ever been introduced with the phrase "Hey Writer Girl." *I've decided to start a book group for the bus stop moms,* the text continues, *and even if you don't hang out at the bus stop any more :(you're still one of us! The planning meeting is next week. Please say yes — we need someone like you who knows about literature!*

This calls for more tea. Liz heads back into the kitchen and fills the kettle. She has learned from experience never to text Sherri back right away, especially if her answer is no. Sherri doesn't like *no* and will do her best to jump over a *no* or sneak around it. So what reason for declining can Liz give that Sherri will accept? Does Liz even know why she's saying no?

Pulling a tea bag from its tiny envelope, Liz thinks it's not that she doesn't like Sherri and the bus stop moms; she just doesn't have much in common with them. They've made a profession out of being excellent mothers, and for them failure — or even mediocrity — is not an option. This same attitude extends to their houses, their marriages and their bodies, but most of their considerable energy is focused on their children. And here's where Liz especially doesn't fit in, largely because Kate doesn't fit in and Liz doesn't try to make her. As far as Liz can tell, Kate's a miniature Polly, eschewing unnecessary rules, questioning authority at every turn. She's not so much rebellious as incredulous that the world is run so poorly.

When Kate gets home, Liz is standing in front of her

design wall, rearranging blocks. "You're back!" Liz calls when her daughter bursts into the kitchen, her cheeks rosy, her hair flying loose from its braid. "I guess I didn't hear my phone."

"Austen's mom wasn't at the bus stop today," Kate informs her mother breathlessly. She dumps her backpack on the kitchen table and shimmies out of her jacket. "Austen's grandma was there. She doesn't really look like a grandma, though. She looks like a mom."

That figures, Liz thinks as she turns to the fridge to get out a bowl of grapes for Kate. It surprises her to hear Sherri wasn't waiting for the bus; stay-at-home moms like her don't schedule appointments so late in the afternoon. It's an unspoken rule that from two-thirty until the last dinner dish is put in the dishwasher, you must be completely available for your children. And of course Sherri wouldn't give up an opportunity to stand at the bus stop with her mother. The bus stop moms love bringing their mothers to the bus stop.

So where could Sherri be? And why does Liz care? Who is Sherri Wright to her? Nobody, really, just somebody whose house is on the same school bus route as hers.

"Can I have my computer time now?" Kate asks. "I only have L.A. homework, and it's just stupid vocab." This said in a tone that suggests vocab will take all of two minutes to complete.

"You can do computer for thirty minutes," Liz says. "You can do the other thirty after dinner."

Kate scootches out of the room, and Liz reaches for her phone. Now she wishes she hadn't unfriended Sherri. If something has happened, Sherri's many friends would be posting all over her Facebook page. "Let me know what I can do to help, sweetie!" "Sherri, I just got heard you got run-over! I'm praying for you!" Maybe she can do a Google search; if there was an accident, it might have made the local—

She stops and drops her phone on the table, as though it has burned her hand. Does she really hope that Sherri Wright is lying hurt in a hospital? No. No, she does not hope for this. Besides, how would that change anything? Sherri would be magnificent in her pain, and when she was fully healed she'd start a charity fun run for child amputees and hip-replacement patients. Maybe if Dan left her, or one of the girls was caught shoplifting...

Liz falls into a chair. This is bad. Something has gone rotten inside of her. Maybe the problem is that underneath it all, she envies Sherri Wright, envies her perfect, shiny life and her problem-free kids. Liz remembers what she read about envy once—that it's the only deadly sin that doesn't feel good. She has to admit that right now she feels lousy.

With a sigh, Liz picks up her phone, offering a quick prayer that Sherri is fine or will be fine, and then she swipes a penitent finger across the phone screen. *Hi, Sherri*, she texts. *I'd love to be a part of your book club. Thanks so much for asking.*

The reply comes seconds later. *Great! See you Tuesday at 7:30! Did my mom remember to text you that Kate got off the bus? I'm at my sister-in-law's—she's about to have baby number four! Can't wait to see my gorgeous new niece!*

Sherri's street is only four blocks away from Liz's, but it feels like it's in an entirely different neighborhood.

The houses have all been built in the last fifteen years, all of them with open floor plans, vaulted ceilings and huge garages that dominate the houses' facades. The Wright house is at the peak of a cul-de-sac, its front drive steeply ascending to the house. Liz is nearly breathless by the time she rings the doorbell.

Austen Wright opens the door. "Mom! Kate's mom is here," she yells, and then turns to Liz and says, "Won't you please come in? I'll take your coat."

"Uh, sure, thanks." Liz is holding a bottle of wine, which she awkwardly sets down on the floor in order to shrug out of her jacket and hand it over to Austen. Austen takes the jacket and the wine.

"That's kind of for your mom," Liz says. "If you could give it to her."

"I was pretty sure it wasn't for me," Austen replies with the barest hint of sarcasm. "I'll put it with the other ones."

Oh, Liz thinks. So it's going to be *that* kind of book group. She waits for Austen to hang up her coat, and then follows her into the kitchen. "She brought wine," Austen informs Sherri, who's holding court around the kitchen island. "Like everybody else."

"Looks like we all had the same idea!" Sherri smiles brightly at Liz. "I'm so glad you're here. I think it's going be awesome to have a professional in our group."

" A professional?" Liz has no idea what Sherri means. A professional reader? A professional wine drinker?

"A professional writer, of course! You can tell us all about the subtexts and subplots, all the stuff I never really understood in my college lit classes."

"I actually majored in communications," Liz admits.

"I don't know that I'm going to have a lot of insight about subplots."

"Oh, I'm sure that's not true!" Sherri says. She waves toward the minibar on the other side of the kitchen. "Now, ladies, if everyone will get herself a glass of wine, we can take this discussion to the living room."

There are seven women in all, and Liz recognizes everyone except a short, red-haired woman standing slightly apart from the group. After pouring herself a glass of cabernet, Liz goes over to the woman and says, "I don't think we've met. I'm Liz Avery."

The woman looks nervous, as though she's not really supposed to be here. "We sort of do know each other. I'm Delia. Delia Stokes."

"Mrs. Stokes? The bus driver?"

The woman nods and shrugs, as if to say, yep, that's me.

"I guess it's been a little while since I've seen you," Liz says. "My daughter walks to the bus stop by herself now."

"Kate, yeah. I noticed." Delia seems to relax, maybe because they're discussing her area of expertise. "I think more kids should do that." She lowers her voice. "Some of these moms are pretty overprotective, if you ask me."

"Come on in here, you two!" Sherri calls from the living room. "And bring your phones so we can coordinate calendars."

Delia rolls her eyes at Liz. Liz giggles. Maybe this book club won't be so bad after all, she thinks.

The living room is decorated in modern cozy—big white couches you could sink into and never be heard from again, honeyed hardwoods that glow warmly beneath heathered jute rugs. A crackling fire dances in the fireplace, classical music curls softly from hidden speakers. The moment she enters the room, Liz feels an overwhelming urge to lie down on one of the couches and take a nap.

What snaps her back to attention is the quilt draped across the overstuffed armchair in the corner. Her first thought is that it must be from Pottery Barn; isn't that where people who don't make quilts buy their quilts? But moving in closer, she realizes it's far too interesting to be a Pottery Barn quilt. The colors are bright, bold hashtags — aquamarine, marigold, fuchsia — against a white background, the quilting a meandering stipple, rows of happy mittens waving in a variegated purple and gold thread.

Still examining the quilt, she asks Sherri, "Did you make this?"

Sherri doesn't answer right away. When Liz turns to look at her, she's surprised by the expression of — what? Discomfort? Distress? — on Sherri's face. Finally Sherri sighs and says, "My sister made it. Or should I say, my perfect sister made it."

"What's Sheila up to these days?" Heather, one of the bus stop moms, asks in a knowing voice. "Besides making you miserable, that is?"

Liz sits down next to Delia on one of the white couches and drinks deeply from her wine glass. The idea that Sherri has a sister who makes her miserable — and makes quilts! — is so shocking she doesn't know how to process it.

"Oh, she's blogging every day about her root vegetables and how popular they are at the farmer's market, and how The Hungry Kitchen is buying up all the chèvre she and

Davis are making." Sherri turns to Liz to explain. "My sister has a farm two hours north of here. If you read her blog, it's like she and her husband invented farming. Really, Liz, I'd love to get your opinion on her writing sometime. She seems to think she's the next Barbara Kingsolver, but I think that's taking things a little far. Her blog is *farmgirlquilter-dot-com*. Read it and let me know what you think."

"My mom makes quilts," Delia says, finishing off her glass of wine in one neat gulp. "I never really got it, though. Lot cheaper to buy your bedspreads at Target."

"It is," Liz agrees, not bothering to say that saving money on linens isn't actually the point of quilting. She's not interested in having that argument right now. She wants more dirt on Sherri's sister.

"So is Sheila younger or older?" she asks, thinking an older sister would be bossier and a younger one more convinced she's found the answer to all of life's problems. This Sheila sounds like a mix of both.

"She's my twin," Sherri replies dryly. "If you can believe it. She acts like she's older, though. She just loves to tell me how to live my life. The fact that I don't grow my own vegetables horrifies her. Why should I grow my own vegetables when there's a Whole Foods less than two miles away?"

"I've been going to Trader Joe's lately; the produce is excellent and the prices are so much better," Carla, another bus stop mom, puts in. "Even though the parking there is miserable."

The conversation veers off into a discussion of the merits of Trader Joe's versus those of Whole Foods. Delia, Liz notices, doesn't contribute much. "Not a Whole Foods girl?" she asks the bus driver.

Delia shrugs. "I go to Kroger, like regular people." She pauses, then says, "Do you think we're ever going to talk about books?"

"I don't think so," Liz says. "I don't think it's that kind of book club."

"Me neither. Too bad, because I like to read. Stephen King, Lee Childs, that kind of stuff."

Liz settles back into a nest of pillows and tries to imagine Sherri's sister. Or, more to the point, tries to imagine a Sherri who's not Sherri. Same blonde hair, except pulled back in a braid, maybe, or worn short and kept hidden under a ball cap. Overalls and muddy work boots instead of skinny jeans tucked into black high-heeled boots. She remembers a story Polly told her about growing up on a farm, how once when she was little she had to pull a breeched piglet out of a sow's birth canal because she was the only one with an arm small enough to reach in to get it. She imagines the adult Sheila (looking just like the adult Sherri, of course) carrying the piglet still in its bloody sack over to the mama and starts giggling. Oh, good grief, this is too much fun.

"I think Liz is enjoying her wine!" Sherri exclaims. "Somebody pour that girl another glass."

Liz waves Sherri's offer away. "I think I've had enough, but thanks. I'm just really enjoying myself tonight. Thanks for inviting me."

"You're so welcome!" Sherri sings back. "I'm just glad to have an intellectual in our group. My sister's going to be in town for our next meeting, if everyone's good with the tenth, and I'm going to show you off. She thinks all of my friends are too busy redecorating their houses to have ideas about books."

"Oh, that reminds me," Carla says. "Can someone go with me to the hardwood floor place on Friday? I just can't decide what I want. What do you think about pecan?"

The noise level rises again as the pros and cons of redwood, rosewood and teak are eagerly discussed. Liz rises unsteadily to her feet. She's only had one glass of wine, so it must be the news of Sherri's twin that's making her feel a bit tipsy.

"I better run — I left Kate at home by herself," Liz says, just to see everyone's scandalized faces. The truth is, Kate and Mitch are having a Minecraft marathon tonight, and Liz could stay out until midnight if she wanted. "Text me when you decide on a book."

"Don't forget to read my sister's blog," Sherri says, walking Liz to the door. "I bet it makes you as crazy as it does me."

Liz would bet no such thing — just the opposite in fact — but she gives Sherri the briefest of hugs and says, "Sisters, huh? Sometimes they can ruin your life."

Sherri looks as though she might cry. She also looks like she might be one glass of wine past her limit. "Thanks so much for understanding, Liz. I knew you would."

Liz feels a twinge of guilt. She doesn't have a sister, but if she could construct the sister of her dreams she'd want her to wear overalls and sew quilts, write a blog about growing vegetables on a farm and make Sherri Wright miserable.

The minute she gets home, she pulls up Sheila's blog. It does not disappoint. For one thing, her quilts are fabulous. They're mostly modern, mostly improvised. Sheila clearly has a great eye. So many improvised quilts strike Liz as off-balance, and not in a good way—more in a "what the hell" kind of way. Liz doesn't believe in what-the-hell quilting. But Sheila's improvisations are rhythmical, laid out in loose but observable patterns. It's like she's constantly sneaking up on a traditional idea and then pulling back at the last second.

Liz squeals with delight when she sees Polly's books listed as inspirations on a sidebar. A second later, she has a revelation: Polly should do a quilting retreat on Sheila's farm. She could come in the summer and they could set up big tents in the front yard. Liz can tell from the pictures it's gorgeous, with a stand of oaks and a single, lovely Weeping Willow. There's a word she's heard for what she's imagining—*glamping*. Glamour camping. Oh, my goodness, she thinks, we could glamp and quilt!

Liz goes to the kitchen to pour herself a glass of wine. Leaning against the counter, she imagines how she and Sheila will hit it off at the next meeting. She imagines the bus stop moms staring, mouths agape, as she and Sheila debate the merits of machine quilting versus handquilting. They'll finally understand that they've never really known the real Liz, that she's different from them, not because she has a quirky kid and a messy kitchen, but because she's interesting and creative. She has a life. She quilts!

How funny that Sherri Wright wants to show her off to her twin, Liz thinks, taking a sip of wine. Liz Avery, famous child abandoner and frumpy mom, driver of an eight-year-old minivan. Now she's suddenly a serious writer and intellectual who's going to make a big impression on

Sherri's supposedly hyper-critical twin.

Liz shakes away the thought that Sherri Wright genuinely seems to like her—admire her, even. How can that be? The woman has made it very clear over the years that Liz is not living up to the standards of the bus stop moms—is maybe even a bad mom; at the very least a lackadaisical mom whose daughter, in spite of her obvious intelligence, probably won't get into a good college due to poor parenting.

That *has* been the point of all of Sherri's texts and emails, right? All of her pointed comments? That Liz is doing a substandard job as a mother? Of course that's been the point, she thinks. That's what women like Sherri Wright live for, to judge other moms.

She takes another sip of wine and ignores the small voice in her head that asks, *Exactly who's been judging who?*

When the day finally arrives, Liz decides to drive. For one thing, it's cold and the wind is just one notch above bitter. For another thing, she's decided to bring her latest quilt. She finished it two days ago and is still in what she and Polly call "quilty love." She jokes to herself that she's taking the quilt to book club because she can't live without it, but the truth is she wants to show Sheila what she's made. After all, Sheila inspired it with her marvelous online gallery of quilts. Working on this one, Liz realized that she had been resisting improvising because Polly was so insistent about it. She'd felt limited by Polly's rules that masqueraded as freedom from rules.

But Sheila's quilts seemed to say that Liz could have it all. She could play with abandon and then make order out of her play. She could improvise *and* measure. And now Liz wonders if she'll ever use a pattern again.

Even Kate got interested when she saw her mother pulling strips from her scrap basket at random and sewing them together. She began choosing fabric for Liz, finding the most unlikely matches that she could. "Now *this* is ugly, Mom," she'd said, handing Liz scraps from an orange and brown print and a purple and green batik. "See how that looks all sewn up."

Polly had shrieked when Liz showed her the quilt via Skype on Sunday. "You've converted! I'm so proud."

"It was seeing those quilts Sherri's sister made," Liz said. "They made me understand better what you've been doing all these years. I told you Sheila's a Pollymorph, right?" Pollymorphs were what Polly's fans called themselves.

"You told me that she has my books listed on her blog," Polly said. "She's not really a Pollymorph until she makes me something. Did I tell you someone sent me a set of four quilted placemats, each one with my face on it?"

"That's a little creepy," Liz replied. "Remind me to never get famous."

"Well, if you do, never give out your address at a seminar, that's my advice."

Driving to Sherri's house, Liz wonders if she should leave the quilt in the car or take it inside with her. She thinks it would be too weird to parade into the middle of the living room carrying a quilt. Maybe to keep things simple she'll bring the tote with her and leave it with her purse in the hallway. That way, if the opportunity comes up, she can grab the quilt and show it to Sheila.

But when Austen opens the front door, she notices the

quilt right away and gives a little shriek. "Did you bring that to make my mom go crazy?"

Liz feigns confusion. "What? Wow! I didn't even realize I'd grabbed that. I had it in the car for a meeting tomorrow."

"A quilt meeting?" Austen asks.

"Uh huh," Liz lies, nodding. "A guild meeting."

"Well, don't let Mom see it. She and Aunt Sheila had a huge fight about quilts today. Last summer Aunt Sheila made quilts for our beds. Except Mom hated them. She said they looked worse than if a kindergartener had tried to make quilts."

"So they're not on your beds?"

Austen glances behind her to make sure no one is in the hallway listening. "Mom gave them to Good Will. When Aunt Sheila found out this afternoon, she was like this." Austen rolls her eyes, sticks out her tongue and shakes her head all around. "Like bizarro crazy."

"Sounds like a fun afternoon."

"It was, after Dad took us to Loco Pops so Mom could rest before everybody came over. Have you been there? I had a Chai Latte pop. It was awesome."

"Is that you, Liz?" Sherri comes into the hallway from the kitchen. "Come meet my sister!" She smiles conspiratorially. "I think you'll find her *very* interesting."

Liz follows Sherri into the living room. Carla and Heather are already here. A little to Liz's surprise, so is Delia Stokes. Delia is sitting in a rocking chair by the fireplace, a glass of wine in hand. Liz had forgotten all about Delia Stokes in her excitement about Sherri's sister, who she sees now curled up on one of the white couches, feet tucked beneath her, telling Heather about homemade yogurt. She couldn't possibly be anyone else; the resemblance to Sherri is almost frightening. How did people ever tell them apart when they were younger?

"I know it sounds scary, leaving milk in a warm place, but the bacteria needs the warmth to grow," Sheila says in the patient tone of a teacher. "It's entirely safe, as counterintuitive as that might sound."

Heather frowns. "I don't really like yogurt all that much to begin with it, but it's the only dairy my daughter will eat. I don't think I could let her eat yogurt that hasn't been refrigerated, though."

"You refrigerate it after it's done," Sheila explains. "Really, it's a million times safer than yogurt made in a factory."

She brushes back a lock of hair that has escaped from her ponytail. Like her sister, Sheila is strikingly pretty, but she's done nothing to enhance her looks — no makeup, no highlights, and by the looks of it, very little sunscreen — and the effect is that of seeing an older, slightly washed-out version of Sherri Wright. Sherri Wright as photographed by Dorothea Lange.

Sherri pushes Liz forward a few steps. "Girls, I hate to interrupt, but I want Sheila to meet Liz. Liz is the writer I was telling you about, Sheila. She's a professional." Sherri emphasizes the word *professional* as though she wants to make sure that Sheila knows her friend isn't any old wannabe writer, but a real writer who gets paid.

Sheila looks up and coolly appraises Liz. Suddenly, Liz feels self-conscious; is she dressed right? She's wearing an oversized blue oxford shirt, jeans and her red cowboy boots, the ones Polly gave her when she turned forty. It's a look that she thinks of as being vaguely artsy and bohemian, but not in an obnoxious way.

"Hey," Sheila says after she's finished looking Liz up and down. "Sherri's gone on about you all day. She's your biggest fan."

"I am!" Sherri exclaims. "I always read Liz's articles in *City Magazine* first. She writes about such interesting things. She had a great article about farm-to-table restaurants in September. I think Dan and I have eaten at every one of those restaurants, just because Liz recommended them."

Sheila nods. "Farm-to-table was big a few years ago. Of course these days a lot of places are growing their own produce. Rooftop gardening is huge. I'm doing a ton of consulting work right now."

"I just write the articles I'm assigned," Liz says with a shrug. "Whether or not they're timely is out of my hands."

"I think all of your articles are timely, Liz," Sherri chimes in. "Farm-to-table is still a pretty new concept around here."

"Sure," Sheila agrees amiably. "Around here. That makes sense."

"Sherri gave me the link to your blog," Liz says. "She thought I might enjoy your writing. But I didn't realize you were such a serious quilter. I love what you're doing with improv piecing."

Sheila raises an eyebrow. "Do you quilt?"

"I do, and your quilts have really inspired me."

"Thanks, Liz, that's so nice to hear," Sheila says, touching her hand to her heart as though she's truly moved. "And when you finish your quilts, do you give them to Good

Will? I hear that's what some people do with quilts."

"Uh, no, mostly I give them to friends. And keep some, too, of course."

"I already told you it was a mistake! I didn't meant to give them to Good Will!" Sherri interrupts. "They were in the attic next to a box of Good Will stuff, and Dan got confused. He made a mistake."

"An honest mistake, right?" Sheila's voice is acid. "Because he knows how much you loved those quilts."

"You know I don't like — I don't like crazy stuff," Sherri says, sounding near tears. "I don't like chaos."

Liz knows she should stay out of this, but she can't. "Sheila's quilts aren't that chaotic, though, not if you really look at them. There's a pattern to her improvisations." She turns to Sheila. "My best friend is Polly Arora; you've got her books in the inspirations section of your blog."

Sheila's expression suggests she doesn't quite know what to do with this information. Finally she says, "I took a class from Polly once. So are you saying you think my quilts are derivative?"

"Not at all!" Liz feels her face flush. "Your work leans way more traditional than Polly's."

"Some people think I'm riding on Polly's coattails. I've had comments on the blog. But to be honest — and no offense, since she's your friend — what Polly's doing isn't really all that new."

Liz wishes she had a glass of wine. There's something about Sheila that makes her feel unbalanced. It's like she's friendly — but she's not. She seems to be passing judgment and withholding it at the same time. The only thing that's clear is she's mad as hell about her quilts being sent to

Good Will, which Liz totally understands. But anyone looking around Sherri's house would know she's not the wonky-improv type. The hash-tag quilt in the living room is as wild as Sherri gets. Sheila must know that, right?

"To be honest," Sheila continues when Liz doesn't reply, "the only reason I have Polly's books on my site is to draw traffic when people do searches on her."

"So you don't actually like her quilts?" Liz asks.

At first Sheila looks taken aback by Liz's question. But after a moment, she shakes her head and sighs. "No, that's not what I meant... I'm sorry. I feel like everything I've said today has come out the wrong way. Listen, why don't we have lunch tomorrow before I head back up to the farm? I'd love to talk quilts with you when I'm feeling a bit more coherent." She turns to Sherri. "Maybe between the two of us, we can convince my darling sister that a little chaos is a good thing."

Sherri's face lights up. "Oh, I think that would be wonderful—lunch that is, not chaos!"

Everyone laughs and begins to talk all at once, relief humming beneath the chatter. Only Delia Stokes looks skeptical. She catches Liz's eye and slowly nods her head, as if to say, *Just you wait—this isn't over yet.*

"We're over here!" Sherri calls to Liz when she enters the crowded restaurant the next day. She's sitting across the table from her sister, and the two women look happy enough, to Liz's relief. She realized driving over that she was nervous about this lunch. What if Sherri and Sheila spend the entire time arguing over the Good Will quilts, with Liz as referee?

"I ordered you a drink—I hope you like peach tea!" Sherri says when Liz reaches the table.

"Um, thanks," Liz says, wondering if Sherri will order her lunch, too.

"I can put that over on the empty seat, if you want," Sheila says, as Liz slides in next to Sherri and shrugs off her purse. Sheila looks a bit more polished today, dressed in a silky white shirt over dark jeans and wearing just a touch of makeup, eyeliner and lipstick, her hair pulled back in a glossy braid. Is that a good sign, Liz wonders, a concession that she's in Sherri's world now and should dress accordingly?

"So tell me how you know Polly," Sheila says as they look over their menus. "I've always admired her, you know. So talented."

"We were thrown together in a suite freshman year of college," Liz tells her, ignoring the fact that Sheila didn't sound so admiring of Polly last night. "It was one of those opposites attract situations—I was boring and bookish and she was a party girl. But we both loved to make stuff. We turned the common area into a craft zone."

"And became friends for life!" Sherri says, her voice sparkling with enthusiasm. "I love stories like that. That's all I wanted when I started college, a roommate to be my best friend forever. Sadly, my freshman roommate was a dud."

"Which is to say she didn't get a sorority bid," Sheila adds with a wink. "In Sherri's circle that meant you were a total failure."

Her tone is light, and Sherri tries to match it when she replies. "That's not true and you know it! You should tell

Liz the story about *your* freshman roommate." She turns to Liz and whispers conspiratorially, "Talk about a match *not* made in heaven."

Somehow they spend the next forty-five minutes telling college war stories over their food — wild roommates, bad boyfriends, mad adventures involving stolen shopping carts and six-packs of cheap beer. Halfway through, Sherri suggests they have wine — "just one glass!" — and she and Sheila end up ordering a split of chardonnay. Liz can't drink during the day without needing a nap, so she declines.

"Do you have any pictures of your quilts?" Sheila asks after she finishes a complicated tale about babysitting her boyfriend's pot plants one spring break. "I've been meaning to ask you that since the minute you got here."

"A few," Liz says, pulling her phone out of her back pocket. "If you really want to see them."

"I do," Sheila says. She gives the serious nod of the slightly inebriated. "I really do."

"Me, too!" Sherri chimes in. "I didn't even realize you made quilts until recently. That's such a nice hobby!"

"Craft," Liz and Sheila correct her at the same time, and then they both laugh.

"I hate it when people call quilting a hobby," Sheila says, taking another sip of wine. "It makes it sound like we're collecting bottle caps."

"Or playing with model trains in the basement," Liz agrees. Her spirits lift. At last she and Sheila have found their common ground — they're both quilters who take their craft seriously. That's all that matters, right?

Sherri makes a pouting face. "Don't gang up on me!"

she says. "I didn't know."

The first picture Liz finds in her camera roll is the recently completed modern Bear Claw. She decides she'll start with this instead of her new improv quilt, which Sheila might think derivative of her own work. "I went back and forth about the binding," she says as she hands Sheila her phone. "I thought about using a batik, but decided the navy blue did a better job of framing the quilt."

Sheila takes the phone from Liz and studies the screen. "I don't know — that navy binding is so visually constricting. A white binding would have loosened this up a little. I see what you're doing here — modernizing a traditional block, but it's not quite modern enough to be truly visually interesting. It's just a little uptight right now."

"Maybe," Liz says reluctantly, disappointed that Sheila doesn't love the quilt. "I guess I see what you're saying."

"Don't be defensive," Sheila tells her, holding up a hand like a traffic cop. "*Uptight* is probably the wrong word. *Conventional* might be closer to what I'm trying to say. And there's nothing wrong with that. This is a perfectly nice quilt. I mean, it's pretty."

Liz has to work to keep her mouth from falling open. Conventional? Liz knows what a conventional quilt is, and her modern Bear Claw does *not* fall into that category. Really, it's not that far from the sort of quilts Sheila makes, quilts that flout tradition while still managing to give it a respectful nod.

So why is Sheila being so awful about it?

Sherri has taken Liz's phone from her sister and now she leans toward Liz. "I think it's beautiful. I wish Sheila had made something like this for the girls."

Sheila laughs. "If that's what you want, you can always go to Pottery Barn. Nobody's stopping you."

Liz finds herself sitting up straighter in her seat. "I don't get it. Why not do something a little more traditional for your nieces, if it makes everyone happy? I've seen your quilts — they have a lot of traditional elements in them, so it wouldn't be a stretch for you as a designer."

Sheila makes a face that Liz recognizes — it's the grown-up version of Kate's *duh, you're such an idiot* face. "I don't make quilts according to other people's tastes."

"But you haven't explained why not," Liz says. She realizes she's shaking. "What could it hurt to make a quilt you know someone will like, even if it's not your style?'"

Sherri places her hand on Liz's wrist. "Sheila's not thoughtful the way you are, Liz. She thinks being an artist means she can be selfish. Not all creative people consider other people's feelings like you do."

Liz ponders this. She'd like it to be true, but she can't recall ever once considering Sherri Wright's feelings. She's never considered the fact that there may be a reason that Sherri works so hard to present a perfect façade to the world, that like everyone else, Sherri is covering up the scratches and bumps of her real life.

Sheila shifts in her seat and then stands. "You know what? I'm just going to take an Uber back to the house and get my things. I've clearly worn out my welcome here. Sherri, I'm sorry for trying to make something for your kids that expresses an original vision. Liz, sorry for being honest about your quilt."

Liz watches Sheila loopily push her way through a maze of tables and chairs to get to the front door of the restaurant and then turns back to Sherri, who is clearly close to tears, the skin around her eyes a splotchy red.

"She's never once been on my side," Sherri says softly when the door closes behind her sister. "No one in my family is ever on my side, really. I've never understood why that is."

She starts to cry, but she doesn't bother to wipe away the tears from her eyes or the trickle issuing from her nose. "My father's worse than Sheila when it comes to being critical, especially when he drinks, which is most of the time. My mother's too scared to say a word. Honestly, some years there's nothing I'd rather do than to skip Thanksgiving."

"Why don't you?"

"Oh, Liz, you're too funny!" Sherri pauses to blow her nose into her napkin. "Thanksgiving pictures aren't any good if you don't have a ton of people in them."

Suddenly Sherri pulls Liz into an awkward hug, and Liz can smell her perfume and a light onion haze of perspiration. Sherri Wright is crying and sweating and getting snot all over Liz's shirt. But Liz doesn't mind. She might not have much experience with perfection, but she's an expert on bumps and scratches.

"You want to go look at some fabric?" Liz asks. "There's a quilt shop at the other end of the shopping center."

"Do you think they'd have that blue material that's in your quilt?" Sherri asks as she lets go of Liz and reaches for her purse. "What did you call that?"

"It's called a batik," Liz tells her. "And I'm pretty sure they'll have it."

"Great!" Sherri says. She pulls a lipstick from her bag.

"What do you say we freshen up first? You could use a little color on your lips."

Liz laughs and takes the lipstick, thinking about the quilts she's going make for Austen and MacKenzie Wright. She sees red and gold Ohio Stars against a navy blue background, with blocks of negative space here and there, each quilt laid out a little differently from the other, each quilt almost perfect, but not quite.

A Quilt for Dr. Wallace

She has waited too long to begin. Lisa knows this now, although until five minutes ago she thought she had all the time in the world.

Two weeks until Christmas, a simple pattern, no special rulers or techniques needed. Just cut, pin, piece, baste, quilt, bind. She has taken two days off work, ostensibly to run Christmas errands and wrap the packages she's sending to her brothers' families in Chicago and St. Louis, but her real plan is to spend big chunks of each day getting this quilt made.

But when she pulls the fabric out of the dryer, she can't remember why she liked it. Why she thought Dr. Wallace would like it. Dr. Wallace is a serious woman who wears cream silk blouses and black skirts under her lab coat. Why did Lisa think a woman like her would appreciate red fabric printed in green and white candy canes?

Lisa throws the fabric in the laundry basket and goes to search her stash. All of her fabric, she realizes, is frivolous. Is flowery, is polka-dotted, is tiny children on tiny sleds. None of it's right for the quilt she wants to make Dr. Wallace, and the pattern she chose in October isn't right, either. Now she can't even remember why she was so taken by the idea of making Dr. Wallace a quilt. Some people are quilt people, some people are duvet people. A subtle but important distinction. Dr. Wallace? Definitely Team Duvet.

Everybody's a quilt person, she hears Carolyn scolding her, and it's almost as if Carolyn's hand is pulling her upstairs to her bedroom, almost as if Carolyn is urging her on, whispering, *Go ahead, get them. That's what they're there for.*

The dresses are hidden on the far right side of the closet, behind the plush terry bathrobe Lisa never wears, behind the size 8 cocktail dress she'll never again fit into but can't bear to get rid of. The first dress she pulls out is the denim shirtwaist. "Old-school suburban mom" was how Carolyn described it, but of course she'd gotten it from Boden, so it was chic instead of frumpy, almost elegant. The second is vintage thrift shop, a cotton shift with large blue and yellow flowers. Lisa had been there when Carolyn bought it, had glanced at the dress briefly without seeing its potential. But when Carolyn tried it on, it turned out to be the perfect summer frock (it helped she was a reedy five ten and looked fabulous in anything).

Lisa picks out two more dresses — the white cotton sundress worn as a cover-up at evening pool parties and another vintage shop purchase, this one a red plaid with a tightly-fitted waist and flared skirt — and decides that's enough for now. Carrying the dresses downstairs, Lisa realizes she's holding her breath. The dresses still carry a hint of Carolyn's scent, a men's cologne called Grey Flannel, soft and subtle, no floral notes, just a hint of sweetness, and Lisa's relieved to find that she can breathe it in without sinking to her knees. When Sam had brought the dresses over in August, she'd backed away from him. "I can't—I can't," she kept repeating, but Sam insisted. "Carolyn wanted you to have them. She said you'd know what to do with them."

Lisa had no idea what to do with them, couldn't imagine why Carolyn had wanted her to have them. But maybe now, here in the middle of December, she does.

Carolyn's been gone over six months, and lately the ache Lisa feels every time she thinks of her friend—well, it hasn't diminished, but it has softened enough to be bearable. Sometimes she even forgets and picks up her phone to text Carolyn. The first time she did this, she spent the rest of the day in bed. When it happened a few days ago, she thought about typing the text—*Ballet moms are the worst, and I say this as a ballet mom*—and sending it, just to see what would happen.

Lisa has her sewing machine and cutting mat set up on the dining room table. When she lays the denim dress on the mat and picks up her rotary cutter, she has to close her eyes for a moment. Is she really going to do this? Can she do it? Why is she doing it?

She has no answers, so she opens her eyes and begins to haphazardly slice up the dress, weaving around the buttons and the pockets. When she is finished with the shirtwaist, she does the same with the shift, cutting it into long strips without use of a ruler, and with the other dresses, too. By the time she finishes the last one, it doesn't feel so much like she's committing a sacrilege.

As she's pinning pieces together, she feels as though she's

in a trance. She has moved beyond improvisational piecing into totally intuitive piecing. She looks over the strips of fabric and *feels it* when she sees two that are meant to be joined together. Sometimes it's two pieces of the shirtwaist, sometimes it's a wide piece of shift married to a narrow piece of denim. When she begins sewing, it's with a certainty she's never felt before. Even when following clearly laid-out patterns, Lisa is the sort of quilter who measures three times before she cuts and reads instructions until she practically has them memorized. She never trusts her instincts, preferring to rely on experts.

She suddenly realizes she's putting this quilt together the way Carolyn would have. That was the beauty — and, she has to admit, sometimes the downside — of their friendship. Lisa is careful, thoughtful, a planner. Carolyn's motto seemed to be "what the hell!" But it worked — they worked — because they shared a raucous sense of humor and a distrust of people who seemed to live perfect lives. It worked because they both hated housekeeping and loved red wine. It worked because they trusted each other enough to be honest. *My kids suck!* Carolyn would text. *Mine are completely unemployable and right now they smell bad*, Lisa would reply.

And Carolyn's haphazardly pieced quilts? Stunning.

Lisa begins sewing pieces to other pieces, sections to other sections. At some point she looks up and sees that three hours have passed. She thought it had been fifteen, maybe twenty minutes.

Annie and Gus arrive home from school at the usual time and Lisa waves them off to the family room, to the TV and computer, tells Annie to preheat the oven to 375 degrees.

"You're letting us having frozen pizza for a snack?" Annie asks, her eyes wide. "But that's what Daddy does, not you!"

"If you play your cards right, we might order pizza for dinner, too," Lisa tells her, and her daughter runs to the family room to tell her brother the good news .

Lisa keeps piecing and the quilt top keeps growing. Jonathon comes home at five-thirty and offers to take the kids out for burgers. Just one more reason to love him, this gentle giant of a man who works so hard to make her happy. "You hit it out of the ballpark when you married him," Carolyn always said, and Lisa rarely had occasion to contradict her.

The top is done shortly after seven. Lisa holds it up, as if showing it to Carolyn. "Very Gwen Marston, don't you think? Very liberated. I think I'm in love with it."

A wave of exhaustion rolls over her. Lisa sits down at the table and buries her face in the top, takes in the familiar scent of her friend. She is crying, but she's also thinking about how she's going to quilt this quilt once she gets it basted. She's thinking about what kind of fabric she'll use for the backing, and how she has a blue and yellow floral print, the flowers tiny and bright, that would be perfect for the binding.

She wonders if Dr. Wallace will love it as much as she does. She wonders if that's why Carolyn wanted her to have the dresses — to remake them and give them away to strangers.

Which is when she orders the flowers.

Dear Dr. Wallace, she writes in the text box for the card that will accompany the bouquet. *Thank you for all you did for Carolyn Russell. She couldn't have asked for a better oncologist. Thank you for the extra year you gave her. Thank you for everything. Merry Christmas.*

She hopes Dr. Wallace likes yellow roses. Because she's not getting this quilt.

The Off-Kilter Quilt

Of the four Bennett sisters, Melissa Bennett was the most sensible, the smartest and the least likely to marry. She was also the happiest. After all, what did she love most in the world? Books, children and quilts, and as the children's librarian at the main branch of the Milton Falls Public Library by day and a volunteer quilting teacher at the community center by night, Melissa spent her life surrounded by the people and things that made her life worth living. A husband sounded nice in theory, but where would she put him?

Her own sanguinity about her singleton status didn't keep family members from playing matchmaker, however, so Melissa wasn't the least bit surprised when she reached the library Monday morning to find her mother waiting for her on the front steps, clutching a napkin that she waved like a flag as soon as she saw her daughter.

"His name is Jim Burke," her mother announced, thrusting the napkin into Melissa's hand. "I met him at a wedding Saturday, and I can't think of the last time I met such a nice man. And he's a reader! A reader, Melissa! Which makes him perfect for you!"

Melissa deposited the napkin in her tote bag with a practiced flick of the wrist. This wasn't the first time her mother had met her before work with the perfect man's phone number scribbled on a scrap of paper, and it probably wouldn't be the last. "It depends on what he reads. Is he a Tom Clancy fan? A Dickens scholar? What are his feelings about the fourth *Harry Potter*? Has he even heard of *Outlander*? The books, I mean, not the TV series. Because I could never love a man who didn't love *Outlander* — the books *and* the TV series, actually."

"Oh, Melissa! Isn't it enough that he reads?"

"If only it were. So am I supposed to call him?" she asked as she started up the steps. "Text him? Send him my resume?"

"Call him, Melissa," her mother said from the sidewalk, a sheen of exasperation coating her voice. "And when you meet him, wear that pink dress you wore to see *Mousetrap*. It makes you look like you have a figure."

Melissa didn't bother with a response. In her thirty-four years, she had never once been at a weight that suited her mother. She'd weighed ten pounds, two ounces at birth, three pounds heavier than Mrs. Bennett would have liked, and then had eventually stretched into a stringbean teen who'd had to endure all sorts of insults about her lack of curves. She'd finally filled out a little in college, but not in a way that drew attention. *Oh, if we could just take Maggie's extra fifteen pounds and put them on Melissa*, Mrs. Bennett was fond of saying, and Melissa and Maggie had argued over many a glass of wine about who should take greater offense.

"I'll call him when I get a chance," Melissa promised her mother as she reached the library's entrance. "And I promise to put on a padded bra before I do."

Mrs. Bennett shook her head sadly and sighed. "I don't know what to do with you, Melissa."

"Invite me over to dinner tonight at six," Melissa told her. "I won't have time to eat between work and class if I'm the one who has to cook."

"Roast chicken?"

"And corn on the cob, please," Melissa said with a good-bye wave. "And potato salad and sliced tomatoes."

"Oh, your father already has some nice tomatoes!" Mrs. Bennett said, noticeably cheering. "So early in the summer, too!" And with that, she was gone, off to find another daughter to genially terrorize.

As soon as she pushed through the library's entrance, Melissa felt the conversation with her mother evaporate behind her. The heavy front doors opened to a bouquet of intoxicating scents, the musty smell of ancient tomes mingling with the perfume of new arrivals and freshly polished black-and-white checkered floors, the aroma of dark wooden tables rubbed down every night with lemon oil.

The library was her sanctuary and the children's room was her playhouse. Who would be at story time this morning? It was the third week of June, the week most mothers and caretakers gave up on their beautifully planned summer days of arts and crafts and backyard play and leaned hard on the library for relief. Melissa could remember being deposited here herself as a child, her mother dropping her off at the foot of the formidable stone steps that led up to the grand entrance.

After grabbing a cup of coffee from the director's office, Melissa made her way to the children's room and happily settled in behind her desk. She took a moment to look over her domain, pleased to see there was a place for everything and everything was in its place, just the way she liked it. Now it was time to check her email and maybe read one or two quilting blogs before the first wave of children rolled in. But wait — was this the latest issue of the *Horn Book* on her desk? Melissa promised herself she'd only read one article from her favorite children's book review, maybe two...

"Miss Melissa?"

Melissa, who had been so lost in her thoughts that she hadn't realized anyone had entered the room, looked up to see Casey Rawlings standing in front of her desk — scrawny, mostly silent ten-year-old Casey Rawlings, her faded pink tee shirt stained with purple popsicle juice, her fingernails bitten to the quick.

"Hey there. Are you here for story time? It's not for twenty more minutes, but you're welcome to go pick out some books to check out. You can use the checkout kiosk. You know how, right?"

Casey nodded and then shook her head. "I know how, but that's not — it's not what I want."

"Did you want to tell me something?"

Casey nodded again, but didn't speak. Oh, the Casey Rawlings of this world! Melissa had met her mother once and clearly the woman meant well. But as she'd immediately confessed, she had a hard time holding down a job or taking care of a child. She'd come into the library to get Casey a card, but one of her many problems was that she lacked a permanent mailing address. "We're in and out of places, depending on whether or not I can get work, you know how that is, staying with this friend one night, the shelter the next..."

Melissa had nodded as though she understood. "I'm sure that can be hard," she'd said. Other than college dorms, Melissa had only lived in two houses her entire life—the house she'd grown up in on Cottage Street, and her own home three blocks away from the library on Orange Street.

"Oh, it's real hard," Samantha Rawlings had agreed. "Especially when it comes to things like this. Here I have a little girl who loves better than anything to read, but I can't get her a library card."

"Do you have relatives in Milton Falls? Maybe one of Casey's grandparents?"

Samantha nodded. "My ex-father-in-law lives over on Hale Avenue. Could we use his address?"

"If he'll come in and sign a paper saying he agrees to it, then yes," Melissa told her, improvising a new library rule on the spot.

Samantha had slapped her hand on Melissa's desk. "Consider it done!"

And sure enough, the next day Casey Rawlings had come into the library holding the hand of an elderly man who smelled vaguely of cigarettes and gin, but who had a friendly smile and was clearly taken with his granddaughter. "This one's a reader!" he bragged to Melissa. "Two, three books a day. The other day I caught her reading the refrigerator repair manual! She understood what she was reading, too!"

From then on, Casey had been a regular in the children's room. There was a beanbag chair in the corner of the reading nest she especially liked, and since school had let out for the summer she'd spent most afternoons cocooned in one of Melissa's quilts with a pile of books in her lap, *The Black Stallion, Because of Winn-Dixie, The Great Gilly Hopkins.*

"What do you want to tell me?" Melissa now softly asked the girl trembling in front of her. "I can see that you're upset."

Casey took a deep breath. "Grandpop died. He was in the hospital all week and then he died."

"Oh, Casey, I'm so sorry." Melissa wanted to reach across her desk and take the child's hand, but she knew Casey wouldn't allow it. "That's so sad."

"And the worst part is, now I can't check out books any more."

Melissa sat back. "Why not? Are you and your mom moving to another town?"

The girl shook her head. "No, but now I don't have an address."

"Oh, I see." And Melissa did see. Not that anyone would swoop down and demand Casey turn her card in, but Casey was an honorable person. If her grandfather no longer lived at that address, as far as Casey was concerned the address was invalid. But the girl needed a library card like a fish needed water. There had to be something Melissa could do.

And of course there was. After thinking for a moment, Melissa said: "I have a plan. You can use my address as your home address. I know we're not family, but we're very good friends, and I *am* the head children's librarian. So I'm willing to take responsibility for you as a library patron, but you have to promise to turn in all of your books on time."

"I always do, don't I?" Casey replied eagerly. "And I never tear pages or eat when I read."

"You take very good care of your books," Melissa agreed. "So all we need to do is pull up your card registration on my computer and put in your change of address."

Casey nodded. "Okay, but can you tell me what your address is? I mean, in case anybody asks or wants to quiz me on it?"

Melissa almost said Casey shouldn't worry, that no one was ever quizzed about library card registration information, but she stopped herself. She could see how important it was to Casey. "Repeat after me: 1505 Orange Street, Milton Falls, Ohio, 44805."

Casey repeated the address solemnly.

"Excellent!" Melissa said, entering the information into the computer. As she typed, she felt a twinge of—what? Worry? Unease? She did her best to bat the feeling away. It's not like she'd wake up some Sunday morning to find Casey and her mother camped out in the front yard. Would she?

Melissa glanced up from her typing. Casey Rawlings was still standing on the other side of her desk, her face shining with undeniable adoration for the head children's librarian of the main branch of the Milton Falls Library.

Oh dear, Melissa thought. What had she gotten herself into?

II.

A buzz of worry followed Melissa throughout the day. As a children's librarian, she'd had her fair share of admirers over the years, but a kid like Casey? She might keep you at arm's length, but she was looking for an adult who wouldn't let her down. Melissa thought of the picture book she read at least once a month to her preschoolers, the one with the baby bird that fell out of its nest and went around asking everything in sight — a bulldozer, a dog, an old car — *Are you my mother?*

Well, she certainly couldn't be Casey's mother, but what could she be? Melissa continued to ponder this as she walked to her parents' after work. A friend, she supposed, which is what she'd always been, since the first time Casey had wandered into the children's section, hungry for good stories and a quiet place to read.

Melissa was famished by the time she reached her parents' house on Cottage Street. Worry did that to her — plus, back-to-back story time hours. "Please tell me dinner is ready!" she called the moment she was through the front door. "I've been dreaming about potato salad all afternoon!"

"Come meet our guest, Melissa!" Mrs. Bennett trilled from the kitchen, and Melissa stopped in her tracks. She couldn't have. She wouldn't! Please say that her mother had not invited Jim Burke for dinner.

Her younger sister came rushing down the hallway into the foyer. "Did you know you were being set up on a blind date?" Ruth asked, *sotto voce*.

Melissa sank onto the bottom step of the staircase. "All I wanted was some chicken and potato salad before I go teach. Why does she do this sort of thing?"

Ruth squeezed in next to her and patted Melissa's knee. "Because she's Mom. Besides, this way is better because you have to leave by six forty-five, right? So even if he's awful, it's a limited window of time and you still get points for being a good sport."

"So? Is he awful?" Melissa whispered.

Ruth shrugged. "He's cute at least. I don't have a read on his personality yet. But apparently he has basic literacy skills and is therefore perfect for you."

"Melissa, get in here!" her mother called. "You're keeping our guest waiting!"

"Here we go," Ruth said, standing and offering Melissa a hand up. "Best of luck."

Melissa checked her watch: 6:05. She could do thirty minutes with Prince Charming. And as irritating as this was, at least she'd have a good story to tell her Quilt Sampler class at seven. *You won't believe the guy my mom tried to set me up with tonight*, she could hear herself saying. *Bald, frumpy, bad jokes. In other words, just my type.*

"Melissa, meet Jim Burke," Mrs. Bennett said when Melissa reached the kitchen, and Melissa once again stopped short. Jim Burke was neither bald nor frumpy. Ruth was right, Melissa thought, reaching out her hand and putting on her best pleased-to-meet-you smile. She could suffer through a half hour of this guy, especially if potato salad was involved.

Jim Burke was sitting at the kitchen table, having a beer with Mr. Bennett. Not only was he attractive, he was dressed nicely, if a little conservatively for Melissa's tastes—khakis and a striped button-down shirt. She bet he was a lawyer. The problem with lawyers in her experience was that they were so concerned with proving how smart they were that they didn't know how to have a real conversation. As a rule, Melissa didn't date lawyers. She also didn't date bankers, because they cared too much about money, and she didn't date engineers, because they were always trying to teach her math.

She wouldn't mind dating a poet, but so far she'd yet to meet a poet in Milton Falls under the age of eighty-five.

"Melissa, this is Jim," her mother announced, practically clapping her hands with excitement. "He's an accountant!"

Figures, Melissa thought, trying to hold onto her smile. "Hi, Jim. I assume you have other interests besides accounting."

Jim Burke shrugged. "That's about it. But when you're as good as I am with a calculator, you don't need hobbies."

Was that a joke? Melissa couldn't tell. If it was, then this Jim Burke had an especially dry delivery.

"Jim was just telling me about a football his grandfather gave him," Mr. Bennett told his daughter, motioning for her to take a seat. "It's autographed by Archie Griffin. Jim's a huge college football fan."

Melissa sat down across from her father. Okay, so Jim did have other interests besides spreadsheets; that was good. Not that she wanted to date him, but at least somebody might.

And he really was cute, she had to admit it, with light brown hair and bright blue eyes. He had that whole boyishly handsome thing going on that some women liked.

Okay, that she herself liked, although she preferred it paired with a slightly more pronounced personality.

"I hate to say it," Melissa told him, "but that name means absolutely nothing to me."

"I wish it meant nothing to me," Jim said, clearly distressed. "Your dad and I were just discussing whether or not I should get the football insured. I'm having a hard time leaving the house without worrying that something's going to happen to it."

"You could take it with you," Melissa said. "Maybe get a special carrying case made for it?"

"Or a bowling ball bag," Jim agreed. "I bowl, by the way. I think that's something you should know about me."

Why? Melissa wanted to ask. What did Jim think was going on here? A job interview? Next thing you know, he'd tell her that his greatest weaknesses were being too organized and giving 110 percent at all times.

"I was on the library science bowling team in college," she offered just to see where it would take them conversationally. "They called me 'The Strike Master.'"

"So you're not just a librarian, but a library scientist?" Again, the tone dry. Could this be a serious question?

"And a darn good bowler, too," Melissa said. "I've got a million tricks up my sleeve."

"Tell her about the quilts, Jim," Mrs. Bennett said, clearly trying to shoo the conversation back on course. "I think she'd be very interested. She's studying for her master's degree in — what is it again, honey?"

"It's a master's in quilt studies," Melissa explained to Jim. "I'm doing it mostly online, through the University of Nebraska."

"So you know about quilts?" Jim asked. "Because I inherited these quilts from my grandmother, and I don't know what to do with them. Some of them she made, others she collected, and I don't know if they're worth anything, or if they — I don't know, have special meaning or symbolism or *what*. I read about quilts being used for the Underground Railroad; what if these are those kind of quilts?"

"That's a myth, I'm afraid," Melissa said. "Although that doesn't mean your quilts aren't interesting or important."

"I have two trunks full of quilts," Jim went on, sounding as though he were confessing a long-held secret. "I'm an only child, and my dad and stepmom just moved to a condo in Florida, so they don't want them. But my grandmother — well, she was my grandmother, you know? She took care of me a lot when I was growing up, and she taught me how to keep a baseball scorecard."

Melissa wasn't inclined to fall in love with Jim Burke, but her heart softened a bit toward this dry, yet oddly emotional, accountant. "I'd be happy to look at them," she said. "You could bring them over to the library, or I could come by your place this weekend."

"Oh, you should get together this weekend!" Mrs. Bennett exclaimed, and Melissa could see the train of thought chugging down the tracks of her mother's brain — an afternoon spent examining quilts would naturally lead to an evening of dinner and dancing, followed by a quick trip to the 24-hour wedding chapel (no questions asked) on Route 96 outside of Ashland. By Sunday, Melissa and Jim would be honeymooning on Lake Erie.

"I can't do it this weekend, I'm afraid," Jim said with a

sigh. "I'm going to Louisville to visit my — my, ah, friend. She's at the Presbyterian seminary there."

Ah, Melissa thought, so he has a, ah, friend. Her mother had clearly not done her homework. "Well, sometime next week then," Melissa said, "or whenever. I'm happy to help you sort your quilts out. Do you know anything about quilts or find them at all interesting?"

Jim leaned across the table toward her, his expression dead serious. "Melissa, before I got my grandmother's quilts, I could not have cared less. To me, quilts were blankets. I'm sorry — I know that's probably offensive to you. But the weird thing is, now that I've lived with quilts in my house for the last six months? I think about them all the time. I even thought about making one. Isn't that strange?"

"Doesn't sound strange to me. I make quilts all the time," Melissa pointed out, checking her watch. "And in five minutes I'm going to go teach a bunch of other people how to make them. You're welcome to join us if you'd like."

Jim appeared to think about this and then shook his head. "I'm not ready. Maybe later. But right now — it's just not the right time."

Well, that was different, Melissa thought as she walked toward the community center. While she felt fairly sure she wasn't going to fall in love with Jim Burke, she could see developing a fondness for him, which wasn't usually the case with her mother's attempted fix-ups. But Jim, well, she felt like she wanted to help him. She wanted to be his friend.

Melissa laughed, remembering that Jim already had a friend, one who he was planning to spend the weekend with. A weekend at a seminary, she reminded herself. Talk about your wild times.

As she made her way down Cottage Street, Melissa passed homes so familiar that she no longer saw them unless she forced herself to look. Sometimes she imagined what it would be like to live in one of the newly-sprouted subdivisions on the outskirts of Milton Falls, with their broad streets and history-free houses. She'd grown up in a Cape Cod on Cottage Street, and now lived two blocks away in a Craftsman bungalow. No one she knew lived in a house that was less than fifty years old. Good thing she liked old houses, Melissa supposed as she passed a sagging Victorian guarded by an ancient oak. Besides, the suburbs lacked sidewalks and she was a walker who preferred to stay off the road.

She wondered where Jim Burke lived and then shook her head. No wondering about Jim Burke! Yes, he was nice and attractive and had what sounded like a very interesting collection of quilts. But even if you took his "friend" out of the equation, what about the khakis and the oxford striped shirt? Who could get swept off her feet by an accountant who dressed like, well, an accountant?

Most of her students had already gathered when Melissa reached her classroom in the community center and were busy at work on their Lady of the Lake blocks, which they'd started the week before. Melissa was setting up her sewing station at the front of the room when Faye, one of her favorite students, walked in with a man Melissa had never seen before.

"This is my nephew, Jordan," Faye explained when she reached Melissa's table, "and he's hoping he can join us tonight. He's an architect — a very accomplished architect, I might add."

Jordan smiled. "Aunt Faye is my biggest fan, which is interesting, since I don't think she's ever seen a single one of my designs."

"I don't need to see them to know you're brilliant," Faye insisted.

"Are you a quilter as well as an architect?" Melissa asked. "I can see how there might be parallels between the two."

"I've never sewn a day in my life," Jordan admitted. "But my firm is assisting with the Milton Falls Heights construction project this summer, and this class sounded like a great way to unwind. Making quilts is just a different sort of building project, right?"

"But one that's less likely to collapse on you if you make a mistake," Melissa said. "Well, find yourself a seat and make yourself at home. Faye can get you started."

Melissa had hoped she might get a little sewing done herself tonight. The Lady of the Lake was a fairly easy block to make, just a center square surrounded by half-square triangles, and they'd practiced their half-square triangle skills last week. But several of her students still needed help, so by the time Melissa finally sat down in front of her own machine, she was surprised to see it was eight-fifteen, time for a break.

"I brought cookies, if anyone wants one," Caitlyn, one the class's teenage quilters, announced, and then added with typical self-deprecation, "They're okay, but not great."

While the class surrounded the cookie platter, Melissa

checked her texts. There was one from Ruth with some thoughts about a quilt she wanted Melissa to make for her and three from her mother regarding Jim Burke. *He's very attractive, if you ask me*, Mrs. Bennett had written in her first text. *And not at all superficial*, she'd observed in the second. *I wouldn't worry about his friend*, the third text advised. *"Friend" doesn't have to mean "girlfriend," you know.*

But it probably does, Melissa thought, and besides, he was an accountant. And a little odd, to boot. She looked across the room to where Jordan was sitting next to his aunt. Now *he* seemed like a perfectly nice and normal guy, she thought. Maybe a little on the young side, but attractive and—

Melissa shook her head. She was being silly. Who had the time? Still, she had to admit she felt a twitch of excitement when she saw Jordan walking across the room in her direction. "I come bearing gifts," he said when he reached her, offering her two cookies wrapped in a napkin. "They're good."

"Thanks," Melissa said, taking the napkin from him. "How do you like quiltmaking so far?

"I'm still learning how to sew a straight line, which is a little humbling for a man who draws straight lines all day, but I'll get there."

"You will," Melissa agreed. "And once you do and then master the quarter-inch seam, the rest is gravy."

"Listen, would you mind if I came again on Thursday?" Jordan asked. "It seems like a great class, and with my fiancé living in Columbus, I have absolutely zero social life right now."

Melissa felt her face redden, as though Jordan knew that only moments ago she'd been sizing him up. "Is your fiancé an architect, too?"

"City planner," Jordan said. "She's working on a big affordable housing project this summer, so she doesn't have time to visit during the week."

Melissa suddenly thought of Casey and her mother. Was it possible they were eligible for affording housing? Or did you have to have a job?

"I understand if you're not taking newcomers," Jordan said. "It's just that this is a lot of fun."

"Oh, sorry—I was thinking about a girl I know who needs a place to live," Melissa said. "I don't know if she and her mother are candidates for affordable housing, though. I suppose you're not the person to talk to about that."

"Probably not, but I'd be glad to ask around. There's some affordable housing attached to Milton Falls Heights, but I'm pretty sure who gets to live there is up to the Housing Authority."

"Of course," Melissa said. "And of course you're welcome to keep coming to this class. It's my job to lure as many people into the cult of quilting as I can. Speaking of which, time to get back to it. Thanks for the cookies."

"Thanks for the class," Jordan replied. "You're a great teacher."

Yes, I am, Melissa thought as she stood to call the class back to order, and great teachers don't have time for romance.

"Okay, everybody— " she began just as her phone pinged. She glanced at the screen, wondering what her mother wanted now. But the text wasn't from her mother.

Jim here, she read. *Great to meet you tonight. Let's talk again soon.*

Someone needs to teach this guy about emojis, Melissa thought. His text had the same flat affect as his speech. "Okay, guys, let's get going again!" she called to the class, before picking up her phone to hit reply. *Nice to meet you, too, Jim. Hope you have a great visit with your friend!*

She hit send and then felt oddly guilty, perhaps because in her mind the word "friend" was in a quotation marks, making it a sarcastic jab that Jim didn't deserve.

Good thing he can't read your mind, Melissa thought, venturing out among her students and their sewing machines.

Good thing she wasn't the least bit interested in Jim Burke.

III.

Thursday morning, Melissa woke up early so she could have a long, leisurely spell on the front porch with her coffee and a book before work. She had toddler time at eleven, and while she loved her rambunctious little pre-literates, the very thought of them could tire her out. Best to start the day with an hour of quiet punctuated only by birdsong and the occasional squirrel dispute.

"Are you coming, Simon?" Melissa called to her cat, who apparently was not. She pushed open the screen door with her shoulder, careful not to spill her coffee, and breathed in the sweet smells of summer drifting from her neighbors' gardens—roses, rosemary and thyme, honeysuckle.

She sat down in her white rocking chair, set her coffee on the table beside it, and opened her book, a Detective Gamache mystery. She loved that these books were as much about the characters as about who done it. Melissa liked a good plot as much as the next person, but if she didn't care about a novel's characters, she couldn't make herself read to the end.

It was mid-afternoon and Gamache was watching a bee scramble around a particularly pink rose when a movement caught his attention, Melissa read, taking a sip of coffee and nearly sighing with contentment. *He turned in his chaise lounge and watched as—*

"Miss Melissa?"

Melissa jumped at the sound of Casey Rawlings' voice and turned to see her standing at the steps of the porch, a hoe in her hand.

"I was weeding your tomato beds out back," Casey continued, "and you should know the squirrels are eating a lot of the half-ripe ones. You might want to cage up your plants. That's what Grandpop always did. Or else spray 'em with wolf pee. My Uncle Wilson in Toledo said that worked for him. You've got to get it online though."

"Casey, what in the world! Wait, wolf pee?"

"Wolves are predators. The smell of their pee scares the squirrels away. You also need to prune some of the branches. They're getting overgrown."

Melissa moved from her rocking chair to the porch's top step. Taking a seat, she patted the spot next to her. "Sit down, Casey. You sure know a lot about tomatoes.

To be honest, my father planted those. I'm not a very good gardener."

"I could tell," Casey said, sitting down next to Melissa. "No offense or anything."

"None taken. But may I ask exactly why you were out back weeding my tomatoes?"

Reddening, Casey shrugged. "I figured if I'm going to use your address, I should help out a little around here."

"I see," said Melissa, nodding. "You know you don't have to, right? I'm very happy to lend you my address without you having to earn it."

"I know," Casey said. "But the fact is, you really could use the help. And I know all about gardening from Grandpop."

"Does your mom know where you are? Is she okay with you coming over here?"

Another shrug. "Sure. I mean she knows that I'll be at the library most of the day. I don't think she cares what I do on my way over there."

"I bet she does care," Melissa said, wondering if this was true. "So why don't you let her know that some mornings you might stop by my house, to help me with my tomatoes? That way she'll have a good idea of where you'll be if she needs to find you."

"She won't, but okay," Casey said. She stood up. "I better get back to those tomatoes. You can get cages at Home Depot, if you want. Or you can go to the garden supply store over on East Main and buy chicken wire. If you do that, I'll build some cages for you."

Melissa watched as the girl walked around the corner of the house before she stood and stretched and then went to collect her now cool coffee. So much for spending an hour reading on the porch. She felt too scattered to read now, and besides, how could she read with a ten-year-old laboring in her backyard? She supposed she had things to do herself, clean the kitchen, fold the rest of the laundry. And she needed to make a sandwich to take for lunch — she had turkey, she was pretty sure, and a nice avocado and some good bread. Should she make a lunch for Casey, too? Well, the girl *was* weeding her garden; the least Melissa could do was feed her. But what if Casey then felt like she needed to repay Melissa for lunch? She'd end up painting the house.

Melissa had just begun to gather up her things when a voice called to her from the sidewalk. "Good morning!"

Turning, she saw Jim Burke, a paper bag in his hand. "Is this a bad time?" he asked, walking toward the house. "That is, if you accept the premise that time can be good or bad. Time's just a unit of measurement, if you think about it. Completely neutral."

He reached the porch. "Hi," he said again. "It's nice to see you."

Melissa felt a bit breathless. "Nice to see you, too. Maybe a little surprising to see you, but nice all the same."

"Here's the thing," Jim said, apparently done with small talk. "I'm on my way out of town, but I'd really like you to take a look at this quilt. I thought maybe it could stay with you for a few days while I'm gone."

"You want me to spend a little time with it, get to know it better?"

"Exactly," Jim said. "So would you like to see it?"

Melissa nodded, and Jim carefully pulled the quilt from the bag and then hung it on the porch railing. Melissa stood to take a closer look. It was a log cabin quilt, its blocks a riot of reds, blues, pinks and browns. "Do you mind if I touch it?" she asked, and when Jim held out his hand as if to say, *Be my guest*, she ran her hand over the fabric — polyester, maybe some cotton blends, so most likely a post-World War II quilt. The log cabin blocks were inexpertly pieced, and many of the strips used to the make the blocks were curved, creating the illusion of movement. Along with polyester, the quilter had used crepe and corduroy, giving the quilt a marvelous texture.

Melissa took a few steps back so she could admire the quilt more fully. How had Jim known this was exactly the sort of quilt Melissa was interested in? Well, he couldn't know that. Obviously. They'd spent a total of, what, thirty minutes together? It was a lucky guess on his part, or else he just happened to have similar tastes to hers, an interest in the funky and offbeat, the not-quite-regular. Or maybe he was just weird.

"I love it," she said, reluctantly turning away from the quilt. "It's really remarkable."

"I think it looks cool."

Casey had returned from the backyard, her face streaked with dirt. "If I ever made a quilt, that's the kind I'd want to make. Is it okay if I turn on the hose out back?"

"Of course," Melissa said. "Just don't forget to turn it off again, please."

Casey's eyes widened. "I would never forget that!" she said as though mortally offended, and then she was off again to the backyard.

"Your daughter?" Jim asked.

"No, my gardener," Melissa said. "She just volunteered

for the position this morning. She's also one of my most loyal library patrons."

"Ah, I've heard of librarians like you. You get the kids hooked on books, and then you make them weed your flower beds."

"Yeah, we're a dastardly bunch," Melissa said. "Although with Casey, it's more complicated. I let her use my address for her library card, and now I'm afraid she thinks she owes me something."

"Why didn't she use her own address?"

"She doesn't have one, I'm afraid. She and her mom are in and out of shelters. She was using her grandfather's address, but he just passed away and she wouldn't think of checking out books under false pretenses."

"So she's trying to pay you back for your good deed," Jim concluded. "Or else she likes thinking of this address as being hers in some way. Maybe she doesn't live here, but she can feel a little ownership by helping out."

Melissa sat down in her rocking chair and considered this. "That worries me a little. I mean she's more than welcome here, and goodness knows my tomatoes could use the attention. But she's got a mother. She's got family. It's not like she's been abandoned."

"There are a lot of ways to be abandoned. Physical abandonment is just the tip of the iceberg."

"Yeah, I guess."

"Give it a few days," Jim advised. "Things have a funny way of working out—or not. In the meantime, you have the tomatoes to look forward to."

Melissa couldn't help but smile. "Thanks, Jim. I feel much better now."

Jim tipped an imaginary hat. "You are more than welcome," he said, and then he was down the porch steps and back on the front walk. "Get to know that quilt a little bit, would you? I look forward to a full report!"

With that, he jogged off, waving at Melissa without actually looking back.

Melissa carefully lifted the quilt from the porch railing and folded it. What a strange morning this had been, with one unexpected visitor after another. Her life seemed to be racking up complications — a little girl she didn't know how to help and a grown man with a quilt obsession and an unclear agenda.

Melissa didn't like complications. She liked things to be straightforward, clearly laid out and understandable. What she needed to do was call Jordan the architect and see what he'd found out about affordable housing for Casey and her mom. She needed to tell Casey she should be playing at the park, not working in Melissa's backyard. And she was going to give Jim's quilt a good look-over right this minute and get it back to him before he left town.

She took a step toward the house. Suddenly the scent of lavender enveloped her. Burying her nose in the fabric, Melissa found herself in Provence, in June, the sun lifting into a periwinkle sky, waves of undulating purple fields…

Goodness! Melissa lifted her head and looked around. What on earth had just happened?

She wasn't sure, but maybe she should hold onto this quilt for a little while longer.

IV.

A week went by, and then two, without Melissa hearing a word from Jim Burke. Maybe he hadn't been able to tear himself away from his seminarian friend. Maybe they'd eloped to Morocco and would be gone for years.

Unlikely, Melissa knew, but if Jim had eloped to North Africa, and possession truly was nine-tenths of the law, then she'd get to claim the off-kilter log cabin for her own. As she'd become more and more enamored of it, this idea made her happy, in spite of the strange ping of sadness she felt when she thought of Jim Burke eating couscous in Marrakesh with his lady pastor love.

The longer she lived with the quilt, the stronger her affection for it grew. How would she live without it? There was only one thing to do and that was to make a quilt just like it. Actually, she decided, she would make two — one for herself and one for Casey. She had wanted to do something for the girl, especially since it didn't look like she'd be able to find her a home.

When had she decided that getting Casey a permanent address was the best thing she could do for the girl? Maybe it was the day Casey discovered the seed catalog in the library, a repurposed card catalog where patrons could leave packets of saved seeds and take home the ones they needed. It was too late in the summer for planting much besides fast-growing herbs, so Casey filled a small envelope with basil seeds and another with parsley and brought them to Melissa's desk.

"I'll plant these by your tomatoes," the girl said, shaking

the little packets so the seeds rattled inside. "I mean, if it's okay."

"You can do anything you want back there," Melissa said. "Have at it."

Casey's eyes lit up. "Anything?"

"Just as long as it's not poisonous to cats."

"I would never poison a cat," Casey said solemnly. "I would poison a snake, but not a cat."

The next morning she was in Melissa's backyard digging, and that afternoon Melissa found her at a table in the periodical section reading gardening magazines, a pile of gardening books by her side. This is a girl who needs a yard of her own, Melissa thought. This is a girl who wants roots.

But it didn't appear Casey would be setting down roots at Milton Falls Heights any time soon, not unless her mother got a decent-paying job, according to Faye's nephew, Jordan. He'd come to quilting class the week before with the news that without steady income, the Rawlings wouldn't be eligible for even the smallest apartment in the new development.

If Melissa couldn't find Casey a house, she could at least make her a quilt, which was her solution to most of life's unsolvable problems. And since Casey had said she'd liked Jim's Log Cabin quilt, Melissa set about copying it. She took photographs and drew a pattern on graph paper. Of course in order to study the quilt, she needed to spread it out on a flat surface, and her bed was the cleanest flat surface she had. It seemed silly to pack it back up only to lay it out again the next day, so Melissa left it where it was.

The first night she slept under the quilt, she dreamed

she was beautiful. There was nothing about her appearance that had changed in her dream; when she looked in the mirror her reflection was the same as always: straight reddish-brown hair tucked behind her ears, hazel eyes, freckles, pointed nose. But she realized for all those years she'd thought herself plain, she'd been mistaken. She was in fact strikingly pretty. Could it be? She walked out of her house and over to the library, which in her dream was right across the street, and sure enough, everyone looked at her and smiled. *Gorgeous*, they whispered to one another. *What a stunning girl.*

She woke up giggling.

Two nights after that she dreamed that the International Quilt Study Center decided to have a special exhibit of her quilts, and all of the *quilterati* were at the opening reception — Kaffe Fassett, Amy Butler, Marianne and Mary Fons, Bonnie Hunter, Alex Anderson, Victoria Findlay Wolfe — oohing and aahing over her creations.

Other dreams came, some fantastical, some just exceedingly pleasant, and Melissa began to worry that now she would never be able to give the quilt back to Jim. Maybe she could buy it from him or convince him to take the copy she was making for herself. Or maybe she could trade him one of her other quilts. There was her hand-pieced Lone Star that had won a blue ribbon at the Ohio State Fair, or her modern orange and white Dresden Plate that had made it into the first QuiltCon.

In practically no time at all, Casey had transformed her backyard. She'd hoed the weeds and mulched the beds, and the tomato plants began putting out new blooms almost immediately. She'd found rocks around the yard and made borders. The basil and parsley sprouted a few days after being planted, and Melissa was surprised by how much the tiny plants pleased her.

She and Casey had fallen into a routine. Casey showed up every morning around seven-thirty and headed straight for the backyard to work in the garden. At eight-fifteen, she washed up and then met Melissa on the porch, where the two of them ate breakfast—usually English muffins with strawberry jam and two strips of bacon apiece—and read until eight-forty-five, when Melissa got ready for work. Casey had taken to doing the breakfast dishes and packing their lunches, and together they left the house at nine-twenty, arriving at the library ten minutes later.

Casey always left the library a few minutes before Melissa did, and Melissa suspected it was to avoid the embarrassment of not being asked to dinner. Melissa wondered if she *should* invite Casey to eat with her, but something always stopped her. It wasn't that she would mind the girl's company. It was just that, well, Casey had a mother, and it wasn't Melissa. Melissa didn't want there to be any confusion on that point.

But now on the nights that Melissa spent at home, nights without classes to teach or meetings to attend or friends to catch up with, the house felt oddly empty. It had never felt empty before. In fact, it had always verged on being overstuffed—with quilts, with books, with sewing machines and comfortable chairs—in a way Melissa found cozy and satisfying. So why did it suddenly feel like when Melissa sat down to sew or read, the other chairs in the room were calling out, *What about me? Who's going to use me?*

The furniture had never talked to her before. Melissa wondered why it suddenly had become so needy.

V.

She knew the day would come, and so it did. The text popped up on Melissa's phone the last week of July. *Can we meet? Can you come to my house for dinner? 1217 East Liberty Street, Friday night, 7PM. Jim.*

Well, what if Friday night *was* bad for her, Melissa wondered? Weren't you supposed to ask first — *is Friday good for you? If not, what nights work next week?*

As it so happened Friday night at seven wasn't bad for Melissa, and so at six-forty she set out for East Liberty Street. She'd briefly thought about wearing the pink dress that made her look like she had a figure, and then wondered why she cared. She could barely remember what Jim looked like. Boyishly handsome, buttoned up. He was the anti-poet, and Melissa had no interest in anti-poets, so she wore a denim skirt and a red tee shirt. She thought about leaving the quilt at home and feigning confusion if Jim asked where it was. *Quilt? What quilt?* Or, *You wanted me to bring it tonight? Sorry! Must have gotten our signals crossed!*

But she knew he wanted to talk about the off-kilter quilt and she felt duty-bound to bring it with her. Her hope was that she could talk him into letting her hold onto it for a little longer. Maybe she'd claim to be writing her master's thesis on it. She'd get it back to him in a year — or a decade — or two.

The address on East Liberty Street turned out to be a small yellow cottage tucked back into a lot that sported a dozen tomato plants, a sprawling collection of zucchini and yellow squash, and a pumpkin vine that encompassed the yard's front borders and boasted one humongous pumpkin.

"I'm growing her for the county fair," Jim told Melissa when he walked out on his porch and found her ogling the massive squash. "Every year I give it a try, but I haven't won yet. Two years ago I got third place."

"That's an interesting hobby," Melissa said. "Unusual, but interesting."

Jim shrugged. "I spend all day with numbers, so it's fun to come home and do something — well, dumb. Mindless, I guess."

"Mindless can be good," Melissa agreed. "Or wordless. It's one of the things I like about making quilts. Sometimes even a librarian needs to get away from words."

Jim seemed to think about this for a moment. "I wonder what pumpkin farmers do to get away from pumpkins?"

Melissa looked at him and cocked her head. "You're funny, aren't you?"

He stared at her blankly. "Funny ha-ha? Or funny strange?"

"Both?"

"I think that's a fair assessment," Jim said. "You want to come in and eat something? I'm making spaghetti with fresh tomatoes. And bruschetta, also made with fresh tomatoes. And I have a bag of tomatoes for you to take home with you. So I hope you like tomatoes."

Funny ha-ha or funny strange? Who could tell? "So I brought back the quilt," Melissa said as she crossed the threshold into Jim's living room. "But I'd be happy to hold onto it a little longer if you don't want it cluttering up your space."

Jim didn't answer. He turned on a lamp next to the couch and another one next to a comfortable-looking leather recliner. "Can I get you something to drink? Water? Beer? A glass of wine?"

"Wine would be nice," Melissa said. "Red, if you have it."

After Jim left to get her drink, Melissa made a tour of the living room. What kinds of books would a pump-kin-growing, quilt-obsessed, tomato-rich accountant stock his shelves with? Founding father biographies? Agatha Christie mysteries? Anthropology? Archaeology? Economics?

"It's mostly poetry," Jim said, returning with two glasses of wine. "I started out college as an English major."

"That was quick," Melissa said. "I'd just begun my snooping."

"I already had the wine poured. Just to be on the safe side."

"In case I'd come in waving a pistol and demanding a class of cabernet?"

"This is merlot," Jim said, handing Melissa a glass. "Are you going to shoot me?"

Melissa shrugged. "No gun. You get to live another day. So, an English major, huh?"

"Yeah, I thought I was going to be a writer." Jim sat down on the couch and kicked his feet up on the coffee table. "Or else a sports broadcaster. But it turns out that what I'm really good at is adding up numbers."

Melissa examined his shelves. There *was* a lot of poetry, as well as several volumes of sports writing by poets and other literary types. He also had an impressive collection of books about Buddhism. On the table by the recliner she found a pile of quilt history books. "You really are obsessed," she said, picking up a copy of *Quilts in America*. "This is a classic."

"My mother died when I was ten, and my grandmother raised me," Jim said. "My father didn't have the bandwidth to take care of a little boy. He gave my grandmother legal guardianship so she could make all the decisions about school and doctors and that kind of stuff."

"Is this her book?" Melissa asked, confused as to what Jim's point might be.

"No. But it's a book she would have liked. She really loved quilts."

Jim stared straight ahead, as though he could see through the wall of the house, beyond the tomatoes and the pumpkin vines, straight into the past that held his grandmother and her quilts and the abandoned boy that he once was. Somehow, watching him, Melissa knew that his grandmother's death had been recent and that Jim Burke was still grieving.

"Tell me about the log cabin quilt," she said gently. "It's a beauty. Did your grandmother make it?"

Jim shook his head. "She found it at a flea market and fell in love with it. 'This one's for your wedding bed, Jim,' she said when she brought it home, but when I got married my wife didn't want it on our bed. She didn't like old things."

"Your wife?" Melissa fell back into the recliner, nearly dropping her wine glass. "You're married?"

"*Was* married," Jim corrected her. "Not for long. Three years into it, my wife — my ex-wife — decided she wanted to go to seminary to become a Presbyterian minister. And I couldn't do it."

"Couldn't do what?"

"Live that life. My dad was a minister and his job pretty much consumed him. He tried to be a good father, but he didn't have time. That's why he handed me over to my grandmother."

Melissa felt dizzy. "So when you talked about visiting a friend at the seminary in Louisville… ?"

"That was my ex-wife. She asked me to do some counseling with her. Sort of a closure thing. It took me two weeks to recover. Are you hungry yet? Because I've got the water boiling and the bruschetta in the oven, so all I need to do is throw in the pasta and chop up a few tomatoes."

"Sure," Melissa said. "But I'd like to talk more about that quilt." And your ex-wife, she thought. And all those books on Buddhism. Whoever heard of a Buddhist accountant?

And then the thought struck her: she'd been sleeping underneath Jim Burke's wedding quilt. She wondered if he'd ever slept beneath it. And if so, had his dreams been wonderful too?

"I was hoping you could tell me something about the quilt," Jim said as they went into the kitchen. "It seems different from the other ones. Fewer straight lines for one thing."

"Does that bother you?" Melissa asked, taking a seat on a barstool by the kitchen island. "As an accountant?"

"Accountancy's just math, and there are all sorts of curves in math. I could tell you a thing or two about curves. But right now I'm interested in the curves in this quilt."

"Well, the curves in your quilt strike me as improvised, which is to say the quilter cut her fabric without rulers, letting the spirit move her. She clearly wasn't using a pattern, but she was inspired by the classic log cabin design. And she most likely used the fabrics available to her — probably from worn-out clothes, or scraps from clothes she'd sewn."

"Which explains the different kinds of material," Jim said. He threw several handfuls of rotini into a pot of boiling water and then looked at Melissa. "I wonder what her name was."

Melissa didn't reply. It was such a marvelous, unexpected thing for an accountant to wonder. For anyone to wonder, really. It was almost as if Jim Burke were a poet. A poet-accountant. Could such an animal actually exist?

"My grandmother's name was Alice," Jim continued after a moment. "When my father dropped me off at her house, he said, 'You're going to live with Alice in Wonderland.'"

"Was it?" Melissa asked. "A wonderland, I mean?"

"In its way," Jim said, peering into the oven. "My garden out front is nothing compared to hers. I think I'm going to give this bruschetta another minute."

"How old were you when you went to live with her?"

"Ten," Jim said. He turned to the stove to stir the pasta. "Ten is a good age for gardening. You're interested in watching plants grow — the science of it, right? — but you're also still a believer."

"In — ?"

"Magic, hobbits, talking rabbits, passageways to fantastical lands."

Melissa thought about Casey making her own magic in the garden. Just this morning they'd made a list for fall plantings — Brussels sprouts and carrots, purple cabbage.

"I still have my ten-year-old gardener," she told Jim. "She's completely reinvented my backyard."

Jim grabbed a purple tomato and placed it firmly on the cutting board. Melissa watched in fascination as he expertly diced it into a pile of tiny, juicy cubes. When he finished, he looked up at her and said, "I've been thinking about it. You should adopt her."

Melissa could feel her eyes widen as though she were a cartoon version of herself. "I'm sorry? You think I should what? Adopt her? But she has a mother."

"Not really, not if she spends all day in your backyard."

"She has a mother," Melissa repeated. "And she doesn't spend all day in my backyard. She spends a lot of her day in the library reading."

"In the library where you work?"

Melissa nodded. "That's where we met. She likes to read."

"And garden," Jim added, julienning a twist of basil leaves.

"She has a mother."

"You could be her guardian," Jim said. "Then she could stay with you. You could teach her how to make quilts."

Who was this man? Just who did he think he was? "You're being ridiculous, and I think I should go," Melissa said, standing. She could feel the heat in her face. She wanted to hit something. She wanted to hit Jim Burke. How dare he! How dare he — do whatever it was he was doing?

"I think we should have dinner and then sit on the porch and admire my pumpkin," Jim said. "We could talk more about quilts. And about why my idea isn't ridiculous. If it were ridiculous, you wouldn't be so mad right now."

Melissa tried to think of something to say, something cutting and sarcastic that would bring this conversation to an end. "You don't know—you don't know what—"

"What I'm talking about?" Jim poured some more wine into Melissa's glass and motioned for her to sit down. "As a former motherless ten-year-old who got to live in wonderland for awhile, I'd say that I do. But we can talk about it. And then you can tell me what you dreamed about when you slept under the quilt. Me, I had a dream about a librarian with a pointed nose who was kind to children, and the next day I met your mother at a wedding and she told me all about you."

Melissa sat down. She took a long sip of her wine. Glancing out the window, she could see bumblebees bobbing among the pumpkin vine's enormous leaves. "Did you think she was pretty?"

"Who? Your mother?"

"No, the librarian in your dream."

Jim nodded. "I thought she was beautiful."

"I guess I could eat something," Melissa said. "But only if there are tomatoes involved."

"It's really too bad I'm allergic," Jim said, peeling a clove of garlic.

"Funny ha-ha?" Melissa asked, leaning forward to pluck a slice of tomato off the cutting board.

Jim didn't answer. Melissa watched in fascination as he minced the garlic into a tiny mound and then neatly pushed it off his knife into the bowl with the tomato and basil. Who would have ever thought that right here in Milton Falls she'd meet a quilt-obsessed Buddhist poet-accountant who on top of everything else could cook?

"Care for some bruschetta?" Jim asked as he pulled a tray from the oven, the kitchen filling with the rich perfume of basil and garlic. Without waiting for a reply, he slipped two slices on a small plate and handed it to Melissa. "Sweets for the sweet," he said.

"I think you mean 'savories for the savory,'" Melissa said, and then flushed. "Not that I'm savory."

"Oh, maybe a little savory," Jim said.

"Okay, maybe a little," Melissa said, biting into the bruschetta. "Oh, my goodness! This is wonderful!"

"Thanks. That makes two of you."

Melissa stared at Jim for a moment and then started to laugh. Funny ha-ha! Or maybe funny-strange? She could see it was going to take her awhile to figure it out. But that was okay. She had all the time in the world.

A Quilting Fiction Q&A with Author Frances O'Roark Dowell

Frances O'Roark Dowell — the bestselling author of *Dovey Coe*, *Trouble the Water*, *The Secret Language of Girls*, and other "beloved books for tweens and teenagers" (NEW YORK TIMES SUNDAY BOOK REVIEW) — first combined her love of telling stories and her love of quilting with the novel *Birds in the Air* in 2016. She hosts the popular "Off-Kilter Quilt" podcast, where she talks about her latest quilt projects with friends and fellow quilters around the globe. Her own little corner of the globe is Durham, North Carolina, where she lives with her husband, two sons, and a dog named Travis. Connect with her online at ***FrancesDowell.com*** and ***QuiltFiction.com***.

Why did you decide to write about quilters?

There's a rule of thumb for writers: Write the books you want to read. I'm so happy whenever writers like Jennifer Chiaverini, Marie Bostwick and Sandra Dallas come out with new quilting novels — I wish more quilters wrote books! So it makes sense that if I love reading books about quilting, I should write one.

What draws you to quilting?

I've always loved quilts. For many years I was convinced that I'd never be able to make a quilt (I'm math phobic, for one thing), and when I finally realized I could, quilting became my new passion. I recently interviewed novelist Marie Bostwick for my blog and asked her why she made quilts. Her answer: "Because I can't paint." I totally got it. Making quilts satisfies my artist soul (the one that can't paint, alas).

How are quilting and writing similar; in what ways do they differ?

With both quilting and writing, I revise a lot. I find this especially true now that I'm designing more of my own quilts. I mess up a lot in both endeavors, but find that sometimes my failures lead to good, unexpected places. Neither books nor quilts always end up being exactly what you intended them to be—for better and for worse. One thing that's different about making quilts is that you're constantly in motion, going from the cutting board to the sewing machine to the ironing board and back again. It's great to move while I'm making something instead of just sitting in front of a computer.

How did the "Off-Kilter Quilt" podcast come about?

I'd been making quilts for a few years when I discovered quilting podcasts. For the most part, these podcasts were homey and conversational, and I loved listening to the hosts talk about their projects and guild meetings, and hearing about the books they were reading and what they were having for dinner. For me, starting a podcast was like joining an ongoing conversation with other podcasters, which then became an ongoing conversation with my listeners, who leave comments, send me emails, and sometimes even come through town and have a cup of coffee with me. It's a really wonderful, supportive community.

# # #

Made in the USA
Lexington, KY
23 February 2018